'What do you ̶̶̶̶̶̶̶̶
Little Miss Pri ̶̶̶̶

'I know plenty about ̶̶̶̶̶̶̶̶̶̶̶̶̶̶̶̶̶ rotten, and your behaviour has done nothing to improve my opinion,' she told him coldly.

'My behaviour. . .?' He sounded surprised.

'You are bone-idle, you have no respect for your family, no idea of commitment. You have wasted your life and think you can use women for your own ends.'

'So that's your considered opinion, is it?' His voice was dangerously low as he slowly moved towards her.

Catherine O'Connor was born and has lived all her life in Manchester, where she is a happily married woman with five demanding children, a neurotic cat, an untrainable dog and a rabbit. She spends most of her time either writing or planning her next story, and without the support and encouragement of her long-suffering husband this would be impossible. Though her heroes are always wonderfully handsome and incredibly rich, she still prefers her own loving husband.

THE PLAYBOY

BY
CATHERINE O'CONNOR

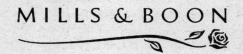

MILLS & BOON

*All the characters in this book have no existence outside the
imagination of the author, and have no relation whatsoever to anyone
bearing the same name or names. They are not even distantly inspired
by any individual known or unknown to the author, and all the
incidents are pure invention.*

*First published in Great Britain 1996
Harlequin Mills & Boon Limited,
Eton House, 18–24 Paradise Road, Richmond, Surrey TW9 1SR*

© Catherine O'Connor 1996

ISBN 0 263 79955 7

*Set in 10 on 12 pt Linotron Times
01-9702-52751-D*

*Typeset in Great Britain by CentraCet, Cambridge
Printed and bound in Great Britain
by Mackays of Chatham PLC, Chatham*

CHAPTER ONE

VANESSA took a deep breath as she caught sight of him. She was tired after the long-haul flight but she knew she could not afford the luxury of a rest. She had to take him by total surprise and on this small island news of her arrival would soon reach his ears, so she had quickly registered at the hotel, leaving her luggage, and set out to find him at once, secure in the knowledge that he would have no idea that he had been tracked down.

'Mr Ryan Searle,' Vanessa said in her crispest tone, her eyes flicking down to the empty beer bottle that lay at his feet; it confirmed what she already suspected about him and she drew a certain satisfaction from the realisation that she hadn't been wrong. 'Mr Searle,' she said louder as the sleeping form remained unmoving, the breathing still deep and steady. Vanessa watched the gentle rhythm of his chest as it rose and fell, her eyes drawn to the strong expanse of naked flesh, smooth and toasted to a seductive golden brown. Ryan moaned softly and shifted in his sleep but he remained dormant.

'Mr Searle!' snapped Vanessa, her voice cracking like a whip across the deserted beach, and Ryan awoke with a sudden jump. He shook his head to dislodge the drowsiness from his brain as his cool grey eyes tried to focus on the unfamiliar figure that had disturbed his much needed sleep.

'Who the hell are you?' he growled, annoyed by the

intrusion. His voice was still heavy with sleep as he swung his strong, muscular legs onto the ground, rubbing his hand over his face at the same time in an attempt to wake up. He groaned as the bright light of the day hit his eyes. 'Who are you?' he demanded again, his voice stronger now.

'Vanessa Mann. I'm here on behalf of the Knight Corporation,' she replied promptly, in her most officious manner.

He awoke then, instantly alert. A bright gleam leapt into his eyes as they flew to hers in quick suspicion. Vanessa's natural instinct for confrontation rose with a sudden rush as she faced him, catching the steel in his grey eyes. He looked at her intently and for a moment she forgot what she was saying. He was a very handsome man, his features clearly defined, his mouth soft but strong.

The photograph certainly didn't do him justice, she thought; it had not caught the very essence of the man, the aura of inner stillness which she knew she had disturbed—and how that pleased her. It was all part of her plan to take him by surprise so that she would be in control of this very tricky situation.

'Oh, I see,' he spat bitterly. 'What on God's earth are you doing here?' he ground out.

Vanessa allowed a smile to touch the corners of her mouth as she gauged his reaction. 'I'm acting on behalf of the Knight Corporation,' she repeated, to make sure he fully understood. She was enjoying the unexpected power she had over him, but it was short-lived.

'You've said that,' he retorted, his voice hard and angry as he rose to his feet with amazing speed. Vanessa stepped back quickly, suddenly aware of his daunting size. She was tall but he was taller, and he towered over her in a threatening way. His expression had changed from one of icy disdain to blatant hostility and unease flowed through Vanessa's tightly coiled body as she struggled to swallow the sick fear and panic that was swelling in her stomach. She had experienced too often how a sudden flare of temper could result in an unprovoked attack on her.

He noted her swift, agitated movement and a flicker of concern scurried across his face.

'Well, Miss Mann...' He emphasised the 'Miss', as if it were a foregone conclusion that she was not married, and Vanessa felt her hackles rise at his assumption. Correct though it was, she felt no shame at her independence—in fact she delighted in it. Yet somehow the very tone he'd used had implied that it was meant as an insult, and for once the knowledge stung her.

She had studied hard to become a professional woman, relying on her wit and intelligence. She had never used her femininity to help her. She had paid a high price once for looking attractive and she wasn't prepared to suffer that shame again.

'I have a document here,' she said, ignoring the jibe, her voice cool and controlled despite the hint of pink that heightened her cheeks. This man was insufferable but he had a quiet power about him, an air of total control that threatened her equilibrium.

'Have you indeed?' he said mockingly, and the sensuous widening of his mouth confirmed that he was, as she had suspected, both amused and unruffled by her words.

'It's simple enough, Mr Searle,' Vanessa managed to say, made breathless by his arrogance and disturbed by the fact that his smile had sent her heart thudding erratically against her chest.

'Ryan.'

Vanessa was confused for a moment, flustered by his sudden change in attitude towards her and instantly wary because she knew that he was a born womaniser; his reputation was legendary and she was not about to become a victim of his fatal charm.

'Ryan,' she repeated carefully, avoiding his penetrating gaze as she spoke. 'It's a simple document that just requires your signature,' she told him, keeping details of the contents to herself; she had no doubt that he would read it with extreme care. Despite his appearance, which suggested he was all brawn, she knew that he was highly intelligent and extremely and expensively well educated.

'There's never been anything simple in a Knight document,' he corrected her in a sneering tone, as if she was a fool to believe that that was a possibility. Vanessa mentally agreed—she had found working for them a tough challenge—but kept a tight lid on her thoughts.

'I can assure you. . .' she began a little nervously, sensing his disapproval and realising that any chance of him signing the document was growing more remote with every second. She could see the raw strength of the man in his bronzed features and it warned her that he was not going to be easily persuaded by her.

'I don't give a damn about your assurances,' he snarled at her. 'I've no intention of signing anything.' There was an underlying tension in his voice which alerted her to his growing impatience.

'The sole purpose of my visit is to ensure your signature on this document,' Vanessa tried to explain, hiding her desperation with skilled ease. Her eyes were as calm as the sea behind her yet they hid a growing irritation.

'Then you've wasted your time,' he told her bluntly, his eyes flicking to her face, causing a fresh glow to cover her cheeks.

'I think you should at least read it,' challenged Vanessa as she balanced her briefcase on her knee and struggled to open it, her feet slipping a little in the soft, warm sand. She felt undignified, out of place on this paradise island in her smart business suit. She felt extremely foolish but couldn't risk losing this opportunity.

'I've no need to,' he retorted brusquely as he pivoted away from her, leaving Vanessa dumbstruck. She snapped her briefcase shut in temper as she watched his lithe body ambling over the sand, striding out towards the shimmering sea. Vanessa marched after him, determined to be heard.

'Wait a minute,' she snapped, furious at his attitude and downright rudeness. He stopped and turned round; the expression on his face told her that her order had taken him by surprise; he was obviously a man who took orders from no one. 'Mr Searle, I insist you read this document. It's of paramount importance,' she told him.

'To you. . .'

'To the Knight Corporation,' she corrected him immediately, her eyes fixed firmly on his, equally challenging.

'I have no interest in the Knight Corporation,' he drawled lazily, his tone one of boredom, but Vanessa detected an underlying curiosity and she took advantage of his admission.

'Then you shall be willing to sell your shares?' she asked, failing to stop a smile of triumph prematurely touching the corners of her lips.

'Sell my shares?' His tone had altered slightly, the change only detectable to Vanessa's sensitive ears.

'They are willing to pay a high price,' she encouraged.

'I'm not selling.' He didn't snap but it clearly took a measure of self-control that was evidenced by the tightening of his jaw not to do so. Vanessa watched him, intrigued by the subtle changes in him.

'You might,' she argued softly. 'Their offer is more than generous,' she went on persuasively.

'Money doesn't interest me,' he told her flatly, the contempt in his voice sharpening his tone slightly.

'Then surely the Knight Corporation does. It is a family concern,' she argued, hoping to touch a nerve.

'Trying to lay a family guilt trip on me?' he asked scornfully, as if the very idea was preposterous, and his mouth quirked into a smile that was totally lacking in humour. 'That won't work,' he said, shaking his head in disbelief.

'I'm not qualified to talk about family loyalty,' admitted Vanessa, then she quickly pulled herself up. It was so unlike her to make such a slip; she kept her background carefully hidden. 'I was merely pointing out that you have a certain responsibility,' she carried on quickly, hoping to cover her tracks, but she noticed the sliver of light that flickered briefly in his eyes and it disturbed her.

'I have no responsibility to that company or family,' he snapped, his voice hard, flat, devoid of all emotion.

'You must have,' countered Vanessa, unable to believe that anyone could have disowned such a prestigious family. She had longed for such security and normality in her own life.

'You have no idea what you're talking about,' he growled. 'So just keep your nose out of my private life,' he tossed over his shoulder as he marched away.

Vanessa watched him with interest; he was totally at one with his surroundings, comfortable in the wild nature of the place that had become his home over ten years ago. She looked on enviously as he slipped off his shorts and waded into the water, diving neatly under a white-topped wave and swimming out into the deeper waters. She would have loved to join him, to forget convention and the reason she was here, but she could not afford such indulgences.

She took a file from her case, flipped it open and began to reread the dossier she had complied on Ryan Searle. She hated having to do this job—it wasn't her style at all—but she knew that if she was successful the Knight Corporation would offer her a permanent position, and Vanessa longed for that security. The file made interesting reading, the sheaf of newspaper cuttings confirming Vanessa's opinion of him: he was selfish and self-indulgent, a womaniser and a wastrel.

Their initial meeting had not gone well but the little Vanessa had seen of him had convinced her that he would not be willing to give up his lazy lifestyle to return to England. She was confident that her new proposals would be readily accepted if only she could get him to read them.

She perched precariously on the edge of the hammock to await his return. The heat of the morning sun was unbearable as it beat relentlessly on her face. Vanessa wiped the beads of perspiration from her forehead. The heat was evaporating her composure and she was becoming more cross with every passing moment.

'You still here?' he said drily when she crossed the beach to join him as he slipped his shorts back on. Vanessa's eyes were drawn to his body; the water still clung in droplets to his smooth, suntanned skin. She followed him as he began to walk away. He did not decrease his pace to accommodate her and Vanessa struggled to keep up with his long strides, her slim court shoes hindering her as her feet sank into the hot sand.

'Obviously,' she returned with a cutting edge to her voice; polite persuasion would get her nowhere with this man, she'd realised. He shook his thick blond hair like a dog shaking himself dry and Vanessa gave a cry of protest as the ice-cold drops sprayed her designer linen suit, marking it with a series of wet spots. He was unrepentant and merely gave her outfit a look of disdain.

'Expensive?' he said, his tone filled with contempt.

'Very,' Vanessa retorted with pride. Unlike him, she had worked hard to achieve a bank balance that allowed her such luxuries and she delighted in being able to indulge herself from time to time.

He shrugged, indifferent to her outrage, and continued walking. A few minutes later they arrived at a wooden chalet which appeared to be where he lived. She followed him into the kitchen.

'You're wasting your time,' he informed her as he pulled open the fridge door. 'I'm not interested in any document. Drink?' he offered, his head still lost in the fridge.

'Have you anything non-alcoholic?' she asked. The doubt in her voice afforded him some amusement and he smiled as he opened a bottle of juice. He passed it to her, his grin wide and warm, white teeth perfect against his bronze skin.

'Pineapple.' He smiled at her, wiping the condensation from the side of the bottle—a gesture that was strangely at odds with the rest of his character, she thought; she hadn't expected such concern.

'Thank you,' she replied, her mouth softening as she took the bottle from him. Their hands touched briefly and Vanessa gave a start, drawing her hand back as if she had been stung. She looked up at him quickly, troubled by the indefinable but delightful feeling that seemed to radiate through her body. The sensation was so alien to her; she never reacted to men—her protective armour was too thick—and yet her heart was pounding dangerously against her ribs just because of his touch.

He saw the confusion that swept through her eyes and a flicker of puzzlement entered his own. His brows drew together briefly in a frown, then it faded, to be replaced by a smile. She lifted the bottle to her lips, glad of the cold liquid because it helped to cool the sparks of electricity which he appeared to create within her. He watched her intently, surprised by her unexpected willingness to drink from a bottle. The comfortable way she held it seemed at odds with her strait-laced image—little did he know that her skill had been born of childhood neglect.

'It's been a pleasure meeting you, Miss Mann,' he

said, his honeyed tone coated in sarcasm as he tossed his empty bottle into the waste bin with practised ease. Vanessa's eyes followed the bottle's path; for some reason which she was not prepared to examine she was pleased that he too had chosen a non-alcoholic drink.

He turned on his heel and strode towards the door.

'Mr Searle!' Vanessa's voice was sharp with worry. She couldn't lose him now; her whole future was at stake here. She saw his step falter momentarily and it gave her extra confidence. 'I've travelled all the way from England; I think the least you could do is look at the proposal.' She hoped to appeal to his better nature, though she was not certain whether he had any good qualities; if he had they were well hidden, she mused.

'I know what the proposal is,' he answered her wearily, not even bothering to turn around as he made his way outside. His steps were laboured; he had obviously heard it all before and found it extremely tedious.

'You do?' she asked, hurrying after him, puzzled. She worked alone; how could he possibly know? Yet she instinctively knew he was speaking the truth; she suspected that he was always brutally honest.

'Robert always lacked imagination; no doubt this is the same proposal he made six months ago,' he told her drily, and waited for the confirmation which he felt sure would come.

Vanessa's eyes widened in surprise and she caught the sudden flare of amusement in his eyes as she asked, 'You received it?' She had been given to understand that he had not received the previous communications. She had made this horrendous trip because of him and now it seemed as if the whole thing had been a complete waste of time, she thought angrily.

'Naturally.' As he spoke his smile widened to a victorious grin that was oddly infectious despite the circumstances. Vanessa, however, remained unmoved; she hated flying but had been forced to make two excessively long journeys to find him and her hopes of being offered a permanent place at the Knight Corporation, as well as her professional reputation, were dependent on the success of this meeting.

'But that's why the company sent me here. We presumed the postal service was unreliable,' she explained, trying to make him understand the lengths people had gone to for him.

But he was too self-centred to care. 'Then you presumed wrong,' he sneered. 'I received it, I read it, I destroyed it,' he snapped at her, each quick and curt word betraying his growing anger with the situation.

'I don't believe this,' cried Vanessa. He had put her through hell because he'd been too ill-mannered to reply to the original proposal. She remembered the painful vaccinations that had left her sick and weak for days and the month's course of malaria tablets which she was still taking. This man was so totally selfish, thinking only of himself and no one else.

'Believe it, lady,' he growled. 'That's why I'm not going to waste my time reading it.' She saw the flare of silvery light in his eyes, bright and dangerous. 'Robert's lack of imagination will no doubt mean this reads the same,' he concluded grimly, his mouth tightening to a thin line of disapproval.

'Do you mean Robert Searle?' she asked, a glimmer of hope sparking deep within her, her heart thudding as she waited for his reply. He saw the look of heightened expectation on her face as the veneer of sophistication cracked a little.

'Yes, he's my favourite cousin,' he said, his voice weighted down with irony, and her eyes widened in surprise. The contrast between the two men was amazing: Robert was always immaculately dressed, in the best that Savile Row could offer. His silk shirts were made to measure, his soft, shining shoes handmade from the finest Italian leather.

Though it was not just their taste in clothes, she thought, studying him with renewed interest and noting the tattered shorts he was wearing. His whole character was the opposite to Robert. Robert was also smaller in stature, with a tendency to put on weight, and his hair was already sparse despite the fact that he was only two years Ryan's senior at thirty-six. No wonder they didn't see eye to eye, Vanessa mused; they were chalk and cheese.

Her eyes flicked back to his face and she felt a sudden flood of embarrassment as she realised that her study of him had not gone unnoticed.

'Finished?' he queried drily, not in the least self-conscious. She knew that men like him were used to the admiring glances of women—not that she was admiring him, she quickly reminded herself, and returned to the safety of business to cover her confusion.

'He has recently become one of my clients,' she began, unable to keep the pride from her voice. It had been quite a coup for her to attract a prominent businessman as a client. 'So if you look at the proposal you will see there have been some alterations,' she ended confidently, pleased that she had managed to persuade Robert to change his mind.

'Really?' he said, responding to the determination in her face.

'I'm totally freelance; I worked on the proposals myself and they are completely different from any others you might have had,' Vanessa explained, realising that she had finally won his attention and determined to keep it now that he was at least willing to listen to her. 'If you would care to look at them. . .'

She wasted no time, perching her briefcase on her knees and flipping it open. Hastily she pulled out the file and extended it out towards him. His fingers had wrapped around it before Vanessa realised her mistake. She stared in horror at her blunder and made a quick grab to retrieve the file.

'No, no, not that one.' She began struggling to offer him another one without releasing her grip on the first file, encumbered by her case. 'It's this other file,' she said, desperation and fear vying for supremacy as she saw his eyes alight on his name. His eyes narrowing on hers warned her that he suspected something.

'It has my name on it,' he commented drily, pulling it from her and flipping it open. Vanessa's heart sank within her; the report was honest but hardly complimentary. He flicked quickly through the papers, his eyebrows raising in mock horror and a smile tugging at the corners of his lips.

'You *have* done your homework,' he said, his voice low and controlled, but Vanessa was an expert at reading emotions and she could see the latent anger despite the half-smile.

'It's just a brief outline,' she babbled hurriedly. 'To

help me understand the person I'm dealing with,' she finished lamely, knowing it did not ring true and that he was certainly too intelligent to be fooled by that explanation.

'Understand the person?' he repeated in mockery, studying her with an intent she found alarming, and her pulse raced as her breath caught in her tightening chest. She faced him with total candour, determined to bluff her way out of the situation. 'You mean so you're able to manipulate them for your clients' benefit because you know their weaknesses,' he accused her, his body stiff with tension.

She seriously doubted that he had any; every inch of the man spoke of his strengths, and not just the physical: he had an inner strength that gave him the ability to laugh at himself. 'Isn't that it?' he persisted sharply when Vanessa didn't answer, being too lost in her own thoughts.

'Not exactly,' she said defensively, trying to keep her voice steady as she was forced to confront his penetrating gaze. The atmosphere was thick with tension as his coolness was replaced by a sudden flare of hostility.

'Then what *exactly* is this about?' he demanded, hitting the back of the file with a sudden rap of his long fingers. The gesture demonstrated his annoyance and Vanessa knew she had to think fast to make amends before she lost his trust completely.

'It's just a profile—information Robert Searle thought would be of some help. . .' Her voice faded slowly away as she saw the anger that firmed his jaw when she mentioned her source of information. His eyes narrowed and temper mingled with distrust shimmered in their depths.

'Then I'd better read it—make sure Robert supplied you with all the salient details,' he informed her, tucking the file under his arm. He was clearly enjoying the discomfort she was experiencing as she fidgeted with her hair. Vanessa knew she had no chance of getting the file back so she shrugged as if it were of no importance.

'And the proposals?' she enquired, trying to keep the desperation from her voice; she would not give him the satisfaction of knowing how much it meant to her. She was certain that if she did it would ensure his refusal.

'Thank you,' he replied, taking the second file, his anger defused as quickly as it had been aroused. Vanessa sighed silently with relief. He gave her a ready smile that heated a dark, cold place in Vanessa that she had hidden away long ago, and she did not know how to respond. The unaccustomed feeling made her heart quicken but her pleasure was tainted by fear. She could never trust men; their emotions were far too volatile, too unpredictable.

'Perhaps we could meet later?' she suggested lightly, forcing a casualness into her voice as she pushed the dark thoughts of her childhood back deep down inside her. A strained smile curled the corners of her mouth; it was meant as a gesture of friendship and she held her breath as she awaited his response.

'You can count on it, Miss Mann,' he replied shortly, the tone sounding slightly threatening, but Vanessa was not easily intimidated; she would never let anyone have that effect on her again.

'I'm staying at—' she began, the smile fading from her face as she resumed her more businesslike manner.

'I know where you're staying,' he cut in, surprising

her for a moment till he continued, 'Thankfully, there is only one hotel on the island.'

She could tell by his tone that he hated the infringement of a hotel marring his paradise, and despite herself she sympathised a little.

'What time can I expect you?' she asked. She wanted to be ready for him; she knew it would be a battle of wits and words, and victory to her meant the chance of being permanently employed by the Knight Corporation. He shrugged, raising his shoulders expressively and shaking his head.

'I don't wear a watch,' he told her simply. 'I've no need of one and that's the way I like it,' he emphasised, his eyes resting on her face for a moment, seeking the disapproval he knew he would find there.

'I'm expected to telephone,' Vanessa replied sharply, her tone reminding him that she was here on business and could not indulge herself the way he obviously did. 'I have to let them know if there have been any developments—'

'Tell them the snake has arrived in the garden of Eden,' he cut in again, and Vanessa wondered whether she would ever be allowed to finish a sentence. She flashed him a look of anger but kept silent; she didn't want to antagonise him unnecessarily.

He turned away, strode up over a sandy dune and disappeared out of sight. Vanessa stared after him, her teeth grinding hard against each other as she struggled to control her tongue. She needed his signature, but once she had that she would tell Mr Ryan Searle exactly what she thought of him.

CHAPTER TWO

VANESSA walked briskly back to the hotel, her swift pace an indication of her bubbling temper. The air was heavy with the sultry aroma of the hibiscus that grew everywhere, their flowers making a colourful carpet among the verdant green.

The hotel was set in its own gardens but it was far too hot to sit outside so Vanessa went indoors, glad of the air-conditioning, which helped to cool her anger. She had seen little of the hotel so far, as she had been so eager to find Ryan Searle as soon as she'd arrived— something she now regretted. But now she had the opportunity to have a real look round.

It was a simple place, but luxurious, and boasted a five-star French restaurant. Tourism had not yet caught on on the island; the poor roads and the lack of a constant electricity supply did not encourage visitors, so the people who came were normally either serious anthropologists or the rich and famous wanting to escape from their usual pressures.

Vanessa liked her room; it was simply furnished but, thankfully, the adjoining bathroom was fully fitted and there seemed to be no shortage of water. She looked at her unpacked suitcase wearily. She never enjoyed travelling and her meeting with Ryan had not gone as well as she had hoped. Her eyes drifted to the bed. It was turned down and the white sheets, cool and crisp, looked so inviting that she decided to rest.

21

She slipped off her clothes and pulled the grips from her hair, ruffling her fingers through it so that it fell like a thick mantle loose over her shoulders. Releasing her hair seemed to release the pent-up tension she was feeling and she knew why. There was something about Ryan Searle that made her tense; he was a dangerous man, she knew that. He aroused a confusion of emotions in her that she preferred not to feel, and yet she felt drawn to his quiet strength.

She only meant to rest for an hour but she soon drifted off into a deep and much needed sleep. She woke with a sudden start; her sleep had been rudely interrupted and for a moment she was disorientated. She sat up, clutching the sheet around her body as she struggled to remember where she was.

'Miss Mann?' The cutting sound of Ryan's voice was accompanied by a sharp, impatient rap on the door that told her it was not the first time he had knocked, and she knew then who had woken her.

'Wait, I'm coming,' she called, her eyes flying frantically round the room in a search for something to put on, but Ryan was in no mood to wait. Vanessa gasped as he flung open the bedroom door and marched in. She sank back in the bed, clutching the sheet up to her naked body as a thin protection against the blazing anger in his eyes. He seemed unperturbed by her state of undress and Vanessa couldn't understand the sinking feeling of disappointment she felt when she realised that he had not even noticed. She launched into an attack.

'I'm not dressed,' she grated, her eyes molten pools of outrage.

He threw her a glance and a hungry interest flared

briefly in the depths of his eyes as he watched the gentle rise and fall of her rounded breasts, which were barely covered by the cotton sheet. His look awoke a deep ache of longing inside her, and she swallowed the pain that welled in her throat as she tossed her head back, facing him with a look of anger and contempt.

'I'd prefer you to leave,' she spat at him, her jaw stiff with tension as she struggled with the vortex of emotion that was swirling through her body, feelings she'd never imagined she would experience. It frightened her. His eyes had never left her face and she lowered her lashes over her eyes before he could read the fear that she knew would be present there. She could not allow him to see her weak and vulnerable.

'I've read this,' he said coldly, his eyes narrowing to hard chips of ice as he towered over the foot of the bed, so close that Vanessa could detect his musky aftershave. She viewed him distrustfully, totally aware of his masculine strength, something that caused painful memories to prick at her consciousness, alerting her to the imagined dangers she always felt in men's company.

'Robert's mind is as twisted as ever, I see,' he commented, his lips curving slightly into a bitter sneer. He tossed the file on her bed, unaware of the turmoil that was raging within her. The newspaper cuttings fell out in disarray over the crumpled bedding and Vanessa's eyes flicked to them; she suddenly found herself hating the numerous girlfriends he'd had.

'Is it?' Vanessa snapped back, angered both by his intrusion and the feelings of vulnerability that he was creating within her. But she couldn't help but be curious, even if that curiosity was mingled with disbelief. She had read the file, knew every detail. The family row which had exploded at his mother's funeral had been well reported in almost every newspaper; was he now suggesting that it was all in Robert's mind? The facts spoke for themselves.

'Correct me if I'm wrong,' she taunted, 'but it was you who hurled abuse at your grandmother and informed the assembled Press that the Knight Corporation was a vindictive company that put profit before people.'

'I did say those things,' he admitted through gritted teeth, his voice a low, dangerous rumble. 'And furthermore, Miss Mann, I stand by them,' he told her, the sudden ring of authority in his tone taking her by surprise. 'And if Robert has managed to convince you otherwise then that's your problem,' he concluded grimly, his eyes fixed to her face.

'Hardly my problem,' Vanessa retaliated. 'The Knight Corporation, however, *is* facing major problems, which is why I'm here,' she threw back at him, refusing to give an inch.

'Really?' he drawled, pleasure warming his voice to honeyed tones.

'Surely you've heard?' Vanessa said, then shook her head. 'No, no, of course not,' she conceded, realising that the London stock market would hardly be of interest here. 'Someone has been buying up their shares.'

'A hostile takeover?' His eyes were alight with sheer delight at the prospect. 'Well, well, well,' he laughed.

'Maybe, maybe not, but it certainly looks like it,' Vanessa said, wondering how deep this man's bitterness went.

'So Robert's panicking; the stupid fool never did have

any guts,' he said, his lips thinning in disgust. 'God, he must be desperate if he's turning to me for help,' he added with humourless honesty.

'He must indeed,' agreed Vanessa. 'The only thing you seem to have any success with is women,' she scoffed in a superior tone.

He picked up on her smug tone and his head shot up, his eyes narrowing on her face, which was still soft with sleep. Her hair surrounded her face in a cloud of vibrant colour, falling in heavy tresses on to her slim shoulders, making her look beguilingly innocent.

'I see you believe all this,' he growled with contempt, pulling his eyes reluctantly from her face and pointing to the file with a long, accusing finger.

'Is there any reason why I shouldn't?' Vanessa challenged, fighting back her fears by attacking. She gave a defiant toss of her head, her anger now matching his. 'You *did* date all those women?' she continued, suddenly feeling a familiar disgust at his antics, which were so typically male.

Her eyes rested on the series of photographs, all showing Ryan with a stunning female draped on his arm, and for some reason that only seemed to fuel her anger even more. She refocused her eyes on him, a gleam of challenge sparking in their blue-green depths. 'And you did refuse to comply with the family's wishes. . .'

'Enough!' snapped Ryan, his voice, quiet but authoritative, cracking like a whip through the tense atmosphere.

Vanessa knew she had touched a raw nerve in mentioning the family rift. It had been a bitter wrangle that had resulted in Ryan coming to the Trobriand

Islands. She knew she would have to be more careful if she was to have any hope of procuring his agreement; arousing his temper might provoke him to refuse.

'I can see you've been given a profile you're happy with so let's leave it at that.' The grim finality in his tone warned Vanessa that his patience was at an end.

'That suits me fine, Mr Searle. Your private life has nothing to do with me. I am merely here to explain the proposals to you,' she told him coolly, hoping to defuse the situation. She wanted him to leave; his very presence caused her heart to thud erratically.

'Then you'd better get dressed and start explaining,' he snarled as he marched to the door, flinging it open and allowing a cool breeze to ripple over Vanessa's body. She gave a shiver, suddenly aware of the heat that Ryan's presence had created within her. She braced herself for the slam of the door but it never came.

She frowned, confused. Despite his obvious anger he had still managed to keep it under control, within certain self-imposed boundaries which puzzled her. The man was a contradiction, passionate and fiery yet with a core of inner composure and self-knowledge that was not easily swayed by emotions.

Vanessa had no intention of rushing; she would not give him the satisfaction of thinking that she was intimidated by his behaviour. This was all a game, a battle, and she was determined to have the upper hand, though the more she saw of Ryan Searle, the more she doubted that she'd ever have that. Robert's profile depicted him as a wastrel and a fool but now that she'd met him she was forced to make a reassessment.

She took a shower, enjoying the cool spray, which washed away the last remnants of sleep and refreshed her completely. She then dressed in a smart apple-green trouser suit and a fine cotton blouse, fastening a thin tan belt around her slim waist and matching it with a pair of strappy tan shoes. She brushed her hair, coiling it back into its neat chignon and securing it tightly.

She looked at herself in the mirror, pleased with the result. She appeared professional again and felt more secure with her image. It made her look in control, but her heart was already racing as she walked back to the foyer area.

Ryan was leaning on the reception desk, laughing good-humouredly with two of the local people. He turned slightly as he heard her approach; his keen, intelligent eyes swept languidly over her and despite all her promises to herself to remain immune to him her heart seemed to flip at the very sight of him. Her own eyes were drawn to his as his generous mouth curled into a sensuous smile.

'Meia and Patimo, I'd like to introduce you to Vanessa Mann from England,' he said politely, and Vanessa extended her hand in greeting, warming immediately to the generous smiles.

'Hello,' she murmured. She felt Ryan's hand on her back, its heat and pressure penetrating her clothing, and automatically she stiffened. She felt so gauche in his presence, and her carefully moulded image of impervious career woman faltered under his steely gaze.

'Have you eaten?' he asked, and his question took her by surprise, although she instantly realised that she was very hungry. Her last meal had been of the cardboard variety on the aircraft, and that had been hours ago.

'No, I haven't,' she answered truthfully, moving her

body ever so slightly to distance herself from his touch, which she found slightly disconcerting. She didn't want to eat with him; that would be too intimate. She wanted to keep this meeting on a safe, professional level where she still maintained some control.

If he noted her reluctance he ignored it. 'Patimo, a table for two,' he said. Vanessa cast him a look of horror; he was still dressed in his usual beach wear, which was hardly suitable for this expensive restaurant. She felt sure his request would be denied, yet Patimo's smile widened even further and he nodded enthusiastically before disappearing from sight.

'Your table is ready,' he said as he reappeared a moment later, and placed a loop of white frangipani flowers over Vanessa's head, the heady fragrance filling her nostrils.

'Thank you.' She smiled, touched by the simple gesture of friendship.

Ryan explained, 'Like the lei given by other islanders, this is to make you welcome. Shall we go through?' he suggested lightly.

It was as if he sensed the awkwardness in her, the fact that she seemed uncertain how to behave. To cover her embarrassment Vanessa lifted the flowers to her face and buried her nose in them. She felt sure that the garland detracted from her professional image but she had no intention of removing it; the simplicity and the generosity of the people made that impossible.

'Oh!' gasped Vanessa in surprise as they walked into the restaurant. 'It's wonderful,' she said, taking in the panoramic view.

The room was large and airy, a huge window running the length of one side of the room giving a full view of the curving bay, the golden sands reaching out into the sapphire-blue sea. The deep green of the forests rose up all around, as far as the eye could see. She moved over to the window to drink in the view. It was breathtaking; the hot yellow sun had changed to a red disc that was sinking rapidly on the distant horizon as if melting into the still sea.

'It's beautiful,' Vanessa breathed. It was so untouched, so natural; no concrete hotels lined the coast, there was no glare of colourful lights, no buzz of traffic or thudding disco music. The only sounds were the calls of the nocturnal animals who were just coming out for the night's hunting.

'Paradise,' agreed Ryan at her side, his warm breath stroking the side of her face, alerting her to his closeness.

She paused for a moment to catch her breath and to steady her thudding heart, then asked sharply, 'An escape from reality?' Her tone sounded more cutting than she wanted it to, but she felt the need to attack him, to force him away from her. Normally her sharp tongue made most men back off.

'No, it isn't,' he said calmly, not reacting to her tone, seemingly indifferent to her caustic manner. He pulled out a chair for her to sit down. Vanessa was not used to the company of men socially and she wondered if he knew how inexperienced she was.

She shook her head to dislodge the unhappy memories that threatened to overwhelm her. Her experiences had made her distrust men, especially those with reputations like Ryan Searle's. Her tension showed on her face but he made no comment, although something told him that he was the cause.

'Out there *is* reality,' he said, his arm sweeping over the whole area. 'Not in here,' he elaborated scornfully as he picked up her napkin, flicking it open and draping it across her lap. Vanessa could not fault his manners; he certainly was a charmer, a real gentleman even though his clothes made him look like a beach bum. Yet his attentions only increased her tenseness and her face flushed with embarrassment.

'I like it here,' she said defensively, enjoying the exclusive surroundings, which were a novelty to her. Vanessa spent her money carefully; she rarely wasted it on going out for a meal. She preferred the luxury of being in her own warm, clean home, safe from everybody.

'That's because you don't know any different; you've never fully experienced anything properly,' he told her as his eyes critically scanned the menu. He tossed it back onto the table. 'It's mostly French,' he said in disgust.

'You don't like French food?' asked Vanessa incredulously, annoyed that he seemed determined to find fault with everything.

'When I'm in France,' he retorted quickly. 'Here I'd prefer to eat more simply.' His eyes rested on her, making her pulse jump, and she hated the strange feeling that stirred deep within her.

'What's so wrong with enjoying the finer things in life?' snapped Vanessa defensively, for she had had so little when she was younger that she now really enjoyed her improved lifestyle.

'Nothing, but it's a wide world and I can see little point in coming to the Trobriand Islands to eat French food in this ivory tower,' he told her, his eyes making a swift inventory of their surroundings. 'You should experience the local food, meet the real islanders, travel round—not confine yourself to the beach and hotel pool,' he told her.

Vanessa was listening with interest; the idea certainly appealed to her. She knew she would never come here again and she would like to see more of the island.

At that point the waiter interrupted them and Vanessa allowed Ryan to order. His French was perfect, as she had expected, since she knew he had spent a year studying in France.

'Your accent sounds flawless,' she said appreciatively, having never had an ear for languages herself.

'I spent a year or so in France,' he said cautiously.

'I know.'

'You do?'

'It's in the profile.'

'Ah,' he commented with a frown.

'What did you study? It didn't say,' she said, merely curious, but a bemused smile tugged at the corners of his mouth.

'Good. I think we should all be allowed at least one secret,' he joked.

'Yes,' Vanessa readily agreed; she herself had so many. 'But you prefer it here, don't you?' she said, skilfully manoeuvring the conversation back to business.

'Yes, I do,' he said emphatically, lifting the bottle of wine the waiter had brought over and offering it to her. Vanessa shook her head quickly; even the smell of alcohol made her queasy and she pulled back in her chair to avoid the sensation.

'So I suppose your answer to the proposals is no,' she

said, her tone resigned, although she hid her disappointment well.

'Not exactly,' he mused, sipping his wine appreciatively, his eyes resting on her face. 'There are some
points I would like clarifying.'

'I'm sure that will be simple enough; the proposal is
more flexible than others have been,' she said, her heart
soaring as she saw the chance to work permanently for
the Knight Corporation come within her grasp.

'There's been a slight shift which I'm curious about,'
Ryan said, his voice as calm and controlled as ever,
although there was a gleam of irritation in his eyes that
Vanessa read as a threat to her future promotion.

'You sound suspicious,' she commented lightly,
hoping to suppress any doubts he had that might
jeopardise his decision.

'I am,' he answered, the bemused curve to one side
of his mouth lifting slightly as he viewed her. But
Vanessa was no longer fooled by his appearance. She
knew that behind the smile was a rapier-sharp mind
and that despite the laid-back dress sense he still
retained the mind of a top businessman. She fought
down the panic that twisted her stomach. She couldn't
lose control of the situation now; her whole future was
at stake and her career meant everything to her. She
had worked so hard to achieve this position and nothing
was going to stop her.

'Maybe I could allay any doubts you have,' she said,
forcing a confidence into her voice that she didn't quite
feel.

'Oh, the draft is simple enough,' he began, initially
calming her fears; but then continued, 'I'm merely

curious as to why Robert should suddenly want my shares.'

'I don't know what the reasons are; the internal workings of the Knight Corporation are not my domain,' she told him crisply. 'Though I should imagine it's in order to fight this hostile bid.'

'And Robert doesn't trust me not to sell them to someone else,' he mused, a secret smile playing on his lips.

'You have made no attempt to hide your feelings about the Knight Corporation; I suppose they thought it best to be assured of your support,' she told him.

'There's something going on and I'd bet a pound to a penny Robert's behind it,' growled Ryan, his mouth twisting into a cynical sneer. 'I don't see why I should oblige him by meekly handing over my shares.'

'I don't see that you have much choice,' Vanessa said as calmly as she could, given that her heart was thudding so loudly that it was thundering in her ears.

His head shot up and he fixed his steely eyes on her, a frown drawing his brows together. 'What do you mean, I don't have much choice?' he snapped.

Vanessa swallowed the painful lump that swelled in her throat. It was obvious that he hadn't read the clauses which she knew would force him to sign his shares over to Robert.

'You have to agree to take a more active role in the business or sign over your shares to Robert,' she explained carefully. 'If you don't agree to either proposal then your grandmother is determined to cut you out of her will. That means you will lose your yearly income as well as any inheritance.'

If the news came as a shock to him he didn't show it,

his lack of response suggesting that the threat of the lack of income was of no importance. His face was a blank mask, though Vanessa sensed an underlying tension in him. He was more interested in what was expected of him, she realised.

'What do you mean, active?' he said, putting his cutlery down whilst he watched her closely.

'You are to return to England and take up your position on the board,' she told him carefully, avoiding the coldness of his eyes.

'Return to England?' he responded, horrified, and a bright gleam leapt into his eyes as he looked at her with contempt. 'How very clever,' he sneered. 'After reading the profile you knew I couldn't possible leave here,' he challenged, his voice containing an odd mixture of admiration and annoyance.

'It was a gamble,' admitted Vanessa, her heart in her mouth as she faced him, and she was surprised when the saw the gleam of respect in his eyes. She hated herself at that moment; despite the fact that it was her job, and she understood that she had no alternative, suddenly the thought of a permanent position with the Knight Corporation did not seem quite so attractive.

'Are you a good gambler—able to keep a poker face?' he taunted, a thin veil of humour covering his anger.

Vanessa didn't answer; her whole life had been a gamble and all her feelings were hidden carefully away behind her poker face.

'I don't gamble,' she said sharply, hating the silvery light that sparked in his eyes; his razor-sharp perception unnerved her.

'Or like alcohol. Quite the Puritan, aren't you?' he jeered.

'I don't need to resort to such futile pursuits,' she snapped back, hating his mocking tone and the personal way the conversation was going.

'Unlike me, you mean.' His tone was icy and Vanessa felt colour rush into her face though she feigned indifference to his remark.

'I'm here representing the Knight Corporation,' she reminded him, trying to steer the conversation back to the safe harbour of business, but he ignored her remark as if she hadn't spoken.

'You look like a Puritan with your hair like that.' He leant across the table, taking her by surprise, and touched the chignon that rested at the nape of her neck. 'It looked so much better loose.'

Vanessa moved her head sharply, her face red. His touch had given rise to a heady desire that was mingled with a gnawing fear. 'Please keep your hands to yourself, Mr Searle,' she told him frostily, though her heart was thudding so fast that her blood was racing through her body.

He withdrew his hand, hearing the coldness in her voice, but continued to look at her intently, studying her with a calm gaze that she found even more disturbing than his touch. 'Let's get down to business, Mr Searle,' she told him firmly, glaring at him.

'Then tell me what Robert is up to,' he demanded fiercely; her reaction to his touch had angered him.

'I've no idea. I'm not privy to such information,' she countered, but the expression on his face told her that he did not believe her. 'I'm a freelance, not an employee,' she protested, wondering if, at this rate, she would ever be. Ryan Searle was the only block, and he seemed reluctant to sign the papers because his distrust of her and his cousin Robert was so strong.

'Then why give you such an important job?' he asked thoughtfully, before his face broke into a wide smile. 'I know; Robert honestly thought I'd be swayed by a pretty face.' And he laughed. Vanessa was surprised. Did she have a pretty face? She guessed not, judging by his amusement, and, although she didn't want to acknowledge the fact, that hurt her deeply.

'I'm good at my job, Mr Searle,' she told him with evident pride.

'No doubt you are,' he conceded graciously. 'But your skill has nothing to do with why you were given this assignment.' He grinned, amused by her innocent expression. 'You're here because you are a woman; little did he know you're a Puritan ice maiden.'

Vanessa stared at him, wounded by the description of her and stung by his assumption.

'If that was your cousin's idea then you are quite correct—he has made a grave midjudgement. I never have nor will I ever resort to deceit and cunning to achieve what I want,' she told him, the heightened colour in her cheeks indicative of her strong sense of discomfort.

'Hardly deceit and cunning, just a little bit of flirtatious fun,' he goaded her, his eyes sparkling with unconcealed delight.

'I have little time for fun, Mr Searle; I'm here on business,' she reminded him coldly.

'We could mix business with pleasure,' he teased, and the colour in Vanessa's face drained as anger replaced embarrassment.

'I see little point in continuing this conversation. If you return the papers to me, I'll go back to England and tell them you do not agree to the proposals,' she said stiffly as she pushed back her chair and stood up ready to leave.

'I haven't said I will not sign my shares over to Robert. In fact you have given me little alternative,' he reminded her grimly, and for a fleeting moment she almost felt sorry for him.

'To prevent it you could return to England to work.' She emphasised the word 'work' as if such an idea would be complete anathema to him. It seemed fair to her; at the moment he did nothing to justify his income from the company.

'I'll think about it,' he said grudgingly. 'Please sit down and finish your meal. I'm sorry if I offended you. No one would ever see you as anything but a professional,' he told her coolly, and Vanessa darted him a swift glance. She wondered whether or not he meant that as a compliment but his face was blank and the depths of his eyes unreadable, though she sensed he was laughing at her.

Vanessa faltered for a moment; she had been enjoying her meal.

'Please.' His dazzling smile softened his firm jaw and it stole her breath away. She nodded, slipping back into her chair, aware of the intoxicating effect it had on her.

'It's just that I know Robert,' he explained. 'And there's something going on at the Knight Corporation he'd prefer me not to know,' he said pensively, toying with his chicken, which had been served in an elaborate style and nestled in a pale cream sauce.

'Maybe there is, but I honestly know nothing about

it,' she snapped, angry that he still did not believe her, and even more angry as she felt that perhaps Robert had not been as honest with her as he should have been. Yet until she'd met Ryan she had never doubted a word he had said; he had always seemed genuine.

'I know, I know,' he said distractedly, cutting into his chicken with a steely precision that reminded her of a surgeon's skill. 'I was just thinking out loud,' he confessed, his eyes resting on hers for a moment, and Vanessa was momentarily silenced by the light that glimmered deep in their unfathomable depths.

'Oh!' she murmured, lowering her eyes and staring down at her meal, hating the fact that she had over-reacted to him. He seemed to have that effect on her. There was something about him that demanded a response from her and, despite her years of training to remain unaffected by other people, her body was reacting without her permission.

'Do you never drink?' he asked, refilling his own glass but this time not bothering to offer her any. He'd noticed the strain that tightened her lips the moment he'd lifted the bottle.

'No.' The answer was curt and abrupt but Vanessa had to prevent the conversation going any further. 'I just don't like it,' she added.

'A bad experience when you were younger? It happens,' he shrugged. 'But once you grow up and have control, know your limitations, then fine wines can be a pleasure,' he explained as he sipped his wine thoughtfully, enjoying its full-bodied flavour.

Vanessa stabbed her fish as if it were still alive and she needed to kill it. Maybe some adults, she thought bitterly, had money to waste on buying expensive wines and maybe they were good but they were not for her. She was too afraid to taste it, too afraid that something in her genes would make her enjoy it and then it wouldn't be quality that mattered, it would be quantity, and she didn't want that.

'What is it?' Ryan's voice cut sharply into her thoughts, bringing her back to the present with a bump. She jumped, startled for a moment. Would she never be free of her past? she thought crossly, determined not to think of it again.

'Jet lag,' she explained hurriedly. 'I've been travelling non-stop for over twenty hours,' she confessed, suddenly realising how tired she felt.

'So how long do you have before you leave?' he asked. It sounded like a polite enquiry but Vanessa doubted it; they both knew why she was here. The document was still paramount in both their minds.

'The day after tomorrow,' she answered briskly, shaking her head at the waiter at his offer of a dessert as he took away her dinner plate.

'So soon,' commented Ryan. 'Coffee?'

'Please,' she agreed. 'The Knight Corporation arranged for the sea plane to pick me up; time is of the essence,' she reminded him, and she could see his mind running over the possible significance of her words.

'That's a pity.'

'Is it?'

She didn't want to fall for his easy charm and if he wanted to flirt she certainly wasn't going to make it easy for him. She didn't know how to.

'To come all this way and see so little of the island— it's a positive crime,' he admonished her, a wicked teasing grin widening his mouth till two creases marked the sides of his usually stiff jaw.

'I've seen the beach and the sea,' she reminded him gently. 'I was positively envious of your swim this morning,' she confessed as she caught sight of the clear blue sea through the window.

'The water is warm; maybe tomorrow you'll join me?' he teased, delighting in her discomfiture, his eyebrows rising, allowing her to see the true colour of his eyes. Grey, certainly, but with a thousand silver shards, reminding her of a shattered pane of glass, and somehow making him look even more dangerous.

'Maybe you could persuade me to sign those papers,' he added, sensing her reservation, her unwillingness to relax.

'I don't think that would be very professional,' she countered, knowing she sounded pompous but knowing also that she was too aware of him, too sensitive to his strong masculinity.

'No, but it would be fun,' he grinned, reaching out and taking her hand, giving it an affectionate squeeze. And although this time she steeled herself against reacting to his touch it made no difference; it was as if a jolt of heat had been forced into her arm, making her feel weak and giddy.

'I don't know,' she answered, shaking her head and drawing her hand away from his light grip, momentarily disappointed when he did not prevent her.

'Whether I sign those papers or not has nothing to do with you. It will be my choice,' he told her firmly, his tone taking on a steely edge that brooked no argument. 'So you might as well enjoy yourself,' he argued logically, his voice softening slightly.

'All right,' agreed Vanessa, surprising herself with her own spontaneity; she never reacted like this. It was a heady feeling, being as relaxed as this, especially in the company of a male.

'Good; now perhaps I should escort you to your room,' he offered, pushing back his chair and tossing his napkin carelessly onto the table. 'You've a lot of sleep to catch up on,' he added with a warm smile.

Vanessa was surprised by his action and immediately cautious as all her doubts and fears about men and alcohol rushed up to overwhelm her. She stiffened at once, her tension making her feel like a tightly strung bow about to break. Her eyes darted to his and she tried to see whether there was a more subtle message in his words. There did not seem to be, but she still rejected his offer.

'That won't be necessary,' she told him, getting to her feet a little hurriedly, revealing her agitation. She wanted to keep their relationship purely on a business level; she had to retain her professionalism.

'Then just to the lift,' he suggested lightly, seeing her distress and accepting that it was due to him but unable to understand why.

She smiled, expelling a silent sigh of relief. 'Isn't this wonderful?' she commented, pausing to study one of the huge paintings that adorned one of the walls in the foyer. Ryan shrugged but his gaze swept over the whole picture, his eyes narrowing critically. Vanessa turned to take in his reaction. 'Philistine!' she cried, looking at his expression and objecting to it.

'I'm not,' he protested, frowning down at his clothes, which certainly gave the impression that that was exactly what he was.

'Do you think they are originals?' asked Vanessa, moving closer to inspect the picture then stepping back to re-evaluate it and bumping into Ryan. 'Sorry,' she mumbled, the words catching at the back of her throat as he steadied her. She moved quickly out of his arms, suddenly aware of how much she longed to stay there and disturbed because of it.

'What do you like about it?' he asked, watching her reaction to the painting with close interest. She turned her head slightly, her profile, unbeknown to her, displayed to perfect advantage. 'It looks kind of chaotic,' he mused.

'Maybe that's what I like; there's an underlying darkness despite the bright colours and the vibrancy of the strokes. I just sense another dimension, something sinister, sorrowful.' She turned, shaking off the gloomy feeling that the painting had stirred within her. 'Oh, I don't know.' She smiled. 'I suppose that all sounds rather silly; I'm no expert,' she added, embarrassed that she had revealed so much of herself.

'They are done by a local artist—a friend of mine; I'll take you to meet him if you like,' Ryan offered.

'Look at that; he has painted a tiny lollipop in the corner.'

'That's right; that's his sign. He never leaves a signature; maybe he doesn't know how to write his name,' he suggested. 'Education is expensive here; not everyone can afford it,' he explained, the hardness returning to his voice.

'How sad,' said Vanessa.

'I think so; with education, who knows what people may be capable of? It's a waste of resources—human resources.' His voice was even sharper now and

Vanessa cast him a quick look, trying to fathom where his anger was directed.

'Still, this painter must have had a wonderful childhood,' she added thoughtfully, unable to keep the wistfulness from her voice.

'What makes you think that?' he snapped, a flare of indignation burning in his eyes.

'I thought the lollipops were a symbol of his childhood; aren't they?' she asked, wanting confirmation, but he shrugged as he turned away.

'I doubt it; the only sweets the children get here are brought in by tourists—hardly a daily event. And I certainly don't remember them playing a big role in my own childhood,' he added bitterly. 'Nanny considered them a threat to dental perfection. She was probably right,' he added quickly with an affectionate smile that failed to hide his pain from Vanessa.

'They never figured highly in my childhood either,' she admitted, pleased that she'd hit on a common bond. 'Not that I had a nanny who disapproved,' she told him, hiding her envy of the lifestyle he had experienced in contrast to her own.

They had reached the lift now. The conversation faded and they stood waiting like embarrassed teenagers on a first date. Vanessa was grateful when the lift finally arrived and the doors slid open. She stepped inside.

'Goodnight, Miss Mann,' he said formally, his attitude and stance totally at odds with the ridiculously casual clothes he was wearing.

'Goodnight,' she answered equally coolly. 'Will I see you at the beach tomorrow?' she asked, wanting to see him again and forgetting all about business for once.

'I'm always there,' he told her, his smile deepening the creases in his cheeks, and as the lift doors closed that final image of him remained in her mind and a gentle smile of her own curled her lips at the corners as she thought of him.

CHAPTER THREE

VANESSA's mind rocked to and fro; she was still unde-
cided as to whether or not she should go down to the
beach and meet Ryan. Part of her so longed to. The
cool breeze that blew up from the shore filled the air
with its salty tang, enticing her to go.

She walked to the beach; it appeared empty; the only
sound was the soft lapping of the white-edged waves as
they kissed the white sands. Vanessa made her way to
the beach bar, where he'd told her he helped out most
days. The door was open and a small window that
served as a counter was propped ajar with a piece of
old driftwood. She paused at the door. The faint smell
of stale beer lingered in the closed area and she could
hear the clinking sounds of empty bottles being stacked
into cases.

'Mr Searle?' she called hesitantly, the intimacy of last
night suddenly seeming strange in the crisp bright day.
She received no answer, and was about to call again
when a friendly face appeared from behind the bar.

'Do you know where Ryan is?' asked Vanessa, but
the man's smile only widened at her words, a frown
puckering his brow. 'Ryan?' she asked again.

'Ryan?' he repeated, then his smile broadened even
further with understanding. 'He's out on beach,' he told
her, pointing towards the sea. Vanessa nodded her
thanks and turned her attention to the wide expanse of
beach, her eyes scanning the whole area. In the distance

she could see a solitary figure, walking aimlessly at the sea's edge. She knew it was Ryan but he looked so alone, so deep in private thoughts that Vanessa wondered whether she should trouble him. She made her way slowly towards him, watching him the whole time, trying to read his mood.

'Good morning,' she said softly as she drew up beside him, her voice low so that she would not intrude on his thoughts. He turned immediately, smiled without surprise, and gave her a long, measured stare before answering.

'Hello; you look better,' he commented briefly as he noted the complete change of clothes. Gone was the austere look of a businesswoman, to be replaced by that of a young woman on holiday. Her cotton shorts and thin T-shirt were ideal beach wear.

'I thought it would be better,' she readily agreed, pleased that he had noticed the change in her.

'Have you put something on your skin?' he asked, concern warming his tone as his eyes ran the length of her bare legs.

'Yes—total sunblock,' she told him, casting her eyes downwards and trailing her toes in the lapping waves, conscious of his gaze.

'A wise precaution.' He smiled, his voice a low rumble that sent a thrill racing down her spine. 'It's going to be very hot today.' He raised his head, gazing up at the sky.

'Hotter than usual?'

'Yes, unfortunately,' he told her, his eyes narrowing against the brightness of the sun. Vanessa caught the trace of worry in his tone; she was sensitive to every nuance in people. She had learnt at an early age that in order to survive one must always be alert, and she was painfully aware of the subtle changes in people's behaviour.

'Why unfortunately?' she asked, enjoying the sunshine after yet another miserable English summer. She liked the sensation of the heat soaking into her skin, warming the very marrow in her bones.

'The weather tends to be a little temperamental; heat like this can often mean trouble,' he said grimly, still seeking the heavens for some sign.

'Trouble?' echoed Vanessa, a gnawing discomfort already stirring in her stomach, her body tensing as she thought of the consequences should the weather change dramatically; she dreaded storms.

'Storms,' he said, unperturbed, but her heart had leapt into action, thudding hopelessly against her chest. Her fear was irrational, she knew, but thunder and lightning had only added to the sinister aspect of that fateful evening. How she hated her drunken stepfather; she knew she would never forgive him. Now every storm made her freeze. She paled as her mind flooded with memories normally too painful to remember.

'There's plenty of warning,' Ryan told her, troubled by the change in her countenance. 'You can always read the signs.'

'Can you?' she asked hopefully, thinking that maybe she would already be gone before the weather changed, back to the safety of her own home.

'I'm not a BBC weatherman,' he laughed. 'But once you have lived here for any length of time you get an instinct about these things,' he explained, but it all sounded a little odd to Vanessa, a bit too hit-and-miss, especially when something as potentially dangerous as a storm might erupt.

'What signs?' she asked, the pitch of her voice rising with worry as she too began to scan the open sea, her eyes straining to find some dark cloud in the clear azure sky.

He waded into the water, turning to her and offering his hand to steady her. She paused, unsure, then allowed her hand to slip into his. There was a reassuring strength in his touch, a warmth that held a security she had never known before, and she waded in after him, surprised by the temperature of the water. It was more like stepping into a bath than into the sea, the water was so soft, so warm and clear.

'See the fish?'

Around her feet swam hundreds of colourful arrows, the tiny tropical fish darting through the clear waters almost oblivious to their presence.

'The storm. . .' he began, then noticed the slight tightening of her grip on his hand. 'If there was going to be a storm,' he began again, his voice, calm and controlled, instilling confidence in her, 'these tiny creatures wouldn't be around; they would have dived for deeper waters, for safety under the coral.' He felt the tension leave her fingers and she withdrew her hand, acutely aware that her grip had tightened.

Vanessa tried to pretend to herself that she simply wanted to waft her hands through the water, feel its refreshing warmth, but deep down she knew that what she really wanted was to cleanse her hand of the searing heat that his touch had once again generated.

'These signs are the result of instinct, then?' she asked, bending low in the water to watch the fish more closely, still aware of his proximity but trying to remain indifferent to him.

'For the animals and fish, certainly, but for the people it is knowledge,' he said firmly. There was a pride in his tone that told her how much the islanders meant to him.

'I see,' she said simply.

'I doubt that; the people who live on these islands are marvellous, and not just at weather-reading—their life-style is just so totally different from ours,' he enthused, beginning to walk along the sea edge, enjoying the feel of the water against his legs.

'It would be. . .' Vanessa considered, looking at the primitive huts that lined the beach further down, but before she could say any more Ryan cut in, his voice sharper now as if he sensed criticism of the place he loved so well.

'True, they lack our development, but their way of life certainly beats ours. Do you know how they judge a man's wealth?' he challenged, knowing that she did not know the answer. 'By the amount he can afford to give away. How's that for a radical concept?' he said triumphantly.

'And you approve of that?' she asked, remembering his family feuds and understanding why he would be at loggerheads with a corporate company.

'Yes,' he answered swiftly, irritation glittering in his eyes. 'It seems an infinitely fairer system than ours.'

'An interesting concept,' agreed Vanessa as they walked along together. 'One you would want to encourage in the Knight Corporation?' she teased, knowing that it would be an impossibility, and she wondered if he was merely paying lip-service to the ideal, interesting though it was.

'If I agree to your arrangement and return I hardly think the board would agree to such a radical proposal. They do have their shareholders to consider,' he told her coolly.

'Wasn't it a disagreement with the board that made you up sticks and run away to this paradise island?' she asked in fun, but she saw the sudden alertness in his eyes and the guarded expression that masked his face.

'Partly, but it was more than that,' he said, and sighed as if even now it still distressed him.

'The broken engagement?' she suggested lightly, and he spun round to face her.

'Have I no secrets from you?' he questioned, with an untroubled smile that warmed her soul.

'I suggest that if you want privacy, Mr Searle, you do not parade your love life through the national press,' she retorted, with an equally charming smile.

'That wasn't by choice; they followed me round, determined to dig up any dirt they could about me.' His tone was light, as if their intrusion had not bothered him, but Vanessa knew it must have taken its toll.

'And you were so obliging, weren't you?' she teased him, enjoying the friendly banter that had sprung up so naturally between them.

'One couldn't disappoint one's public; they wanted a rich, good-looking, intelligent—'

'Humble?' she cut in.

'Good Lord, no; that would never do. I had to be arrogant, cold, aloof, but with a strong sense of fun.'

'And an even stronger stomach, judging by the amount of champagne you drank.'

'Yes, it was all hard work,' he laughed. 'That lifestyle all seems so long ago now, and so far away.'

'I'm sure you could very quickly and easily take up the reins again.'

'No doubt,' he admitted, with a nod. 'I'd have to; it would be expected of me,' he added, his tone lacking the humour it had had before.

'And you couldn't disappoint the Press,' she said lightly.

'I wasn't thinking of the Press,' he told her cryptically.

'Your family forced you to play the role of a wastrel, did they?' she taunted. 'When of course poor you really wanted to be a hard-working member of the family firm,' she said in mock sympathy.

'Things are rarely what they seem.'

'Aren't they? I can remember how distraught your fiancée was—headline news, it was, for at least a week. The wedding of the year called off with only five days to go.'

'It was unavoidable,' he said, stalking away, his body rigid, and Vanessa knew she had touched on a sore point.

'Cold feet?' she asked his back, and she blinked in surprise as he spun round, the expression on his face warning her to say no more.

'No,' he said shortly, before adding, 'My reasons were personal.'

Vanessa could almost hear the shutters going up, the doors closing; the casual conversation had disappeared behind a cold façade of well-controlled anger.

'I'm sorry, I didn't mean to pry.' She was aware that she had made contact with a raw nerve, a private, sensitive place that she had no right to touch, and she regretted it now.

'Didn't you?' he accused her, hitting back—a reaction

Vanessa knew well. 'No, no, of course not,' he said lightly. 'I'm sorry too.' A hint of a smile touched the corners of his mouth and Vanessa knew she had been forgiven.

'It's all right; we're both in a difficult situation,' she said, hoping he would make allowances for her too. She enjoyed his company; whether that was due to the influence of the holiday atmosphere was something she was not prepared to dwell on.

'That's true,' he agreed, and the smile that widened his mouth to a sensuous grin played havoc with her stomach although she managed to present a calm, unruffled face. 'Today is too good to waste on business.'

'Isn't every day like that for you?' she teased.

'It depends on what you mean by business; I told you, I *do* work here.'

'The beach bar,' said Vanessa drily, her tone indicating that she did not consider it a worthwhile occupation.

'I have other commitments,' he told her as they waded from the water.

'Do you?' she asked, her incredulity widening the sea-green pools of her eyes, her dark brows rising in mockery as she faced him.

'Yes, but today, for you, I'm willing to take a day off,' he said, with a generous smile that revealed his even white teeth, their brilliance highlighted by the contrast with his deeply tanned skin.

'I'm flattered,' said Vanessa, inclining her head and allowing a half-smile to touch the corners of her mouth.

'You should be,' he said, halting suddenly and sounding really serious, but his eyes still shone with amusement.

'So what do you have in mind?' she asked, her voice

taking on an unexpected huskiness. She turned away as a pink glow rose in her cheeks; this man seemed to trigger reactions from her that she had no control over.

'First, how about a stroll around the island? We'll have to be careful, though,' he warned, fixing his eyes firmly on her, a slow, gentle smile curving his mouth.

'Why?' asked Vanessa, suddenly a little nervous, and her eyes darted quickly over to the thick dark trees which suddenly seemed to cover a host of hidden dangers. 'I thought the people were friendly?' she added, sinking her teeth into the side of her cheek, feeling a little fearful.

'They are!' he exclaimed, laughing. 'Especially the women at this time of year. It's the season of yam-gathering—an important event in the life of the island; it's the main source of food here.'

'So where's the danger?' queried Vanessa, intrigued yet still unsure.

Ryan seemed amused by her question. 'Should we inadvertently cross the path of the women while they are collecting, they will strip me and send me back to the nearest village so I can be the butt of the men's scorn.'

'Then we shall have to be careful,' Vanessa said in mock seriousness, her face straight, but it wasn't long before the laughter that came so easily to him managed to make her smile. She was not used to laughter, to freely letting herself be happy—

'Very careful,' he agreed, his voice taking on a deeper, sexy tone, and for a fleeting moment Vanessa allowed herself to imagine him naked. She suspected he had an all-over tan—bathing nude here would certainly be no problem... An embarrassed heat covered her cheeks as she realised how far her thoughts might be willing to go, should she let them, and the laughter in his eyes teased her, as if he knew exactly what had been on her mind.

'There's only one road,' he told her as he lifted the branches of an overhanging tree, and Vanessa dipped under the arc of his arm, enjoying the cool stillness of the natural dark green umbrella. 'And I use the word in the broadest sense of the word,' he warned her as the dusty, rutted path came into view.

'I presume it would be best if we walked, then?' Vanessa said as she looked at the poor state of the so-called road; huge holes and an abundance of rocks were scattered everywhere.

'Essential, I'd say.' He laughed easily, catching her arm as she tripped over a stone. 'I've no car,' he added, still holding onto her, and Vanessa looked up at him and he looked deep into her eyes, making her legs suddenly feel weak. She held her breath tight, holding in with it all the emotions he aroused in her when his well-muscled body was only inches away from her.

Finally she forced herself to breathe again, and moved away from him. The movement was meant to be graceful and unhurried but instead she found herself snatching her arm from his, angry at the desire he stirred within her. He raised his palms up in the air in front of himself, as if surrendering.

'Sorry,' he apologised tersely, but his eyes sparked with delight and his lips had creased into a wicked smile of satisfaction. 'Come on,' he said softly, seeing that she was not amused, and he wondered what made her so uptight.

The road wove haphazardly through the trees. The

noise startled Vanessa. A chorus of birds sang incessantly in the high branches, darting from tree to tree, rustling the leaves with their feathers.

'What's it really like here?' she asked. It did look like paradise and she could well imagine someone who had no need to work being perfectly happy here. It was so idyllic.

'The weather is good, the land fertile, the people friendly, but. . .' His eyes clouded with a mixture of emotions that Vanessa found impossible to read.

'But what?' she asked, panic beginning to rise within her again, but the quiet stillness of his presence reassured her.

'Even if I live here forever I don't think I'll ever be more than an outsider,' he said wistfully, allowing Vanessa to see a glimpse of the more sensitive side of him which he normally hid.

'An outsider?'

'Someone of no consequence to them,' he explained ruefully. 'They are an ancient people; they say they are natives of the islands but experts say they originated in south-east Asia by way of New Guinea. That's why there is no typical Trobriandian; their skin colour, size, hair type can vary enormously; some look Polynesian, some Asian, others Negroid.'

She could tell that he was warming to a subject that was close to his heart and she listened with interest as he spoke of the people and their way of life.

'So if these people are so healthy why is life expectancy so low?' she asked as they neared a village and a host of children rushed out to greet them, their faces eager and smiling with the familiar warmth of the islanders.

'Infection,' he said in a sad voice. 'Even the smallest cut can develop and prove fatal. There is also a particularly nasty strain of malaria here—the air, as you've discovered, teems with mosquitoes.' Vanessa knew this all too well—they had been waving their hands continually since leaving the beach to disperse the mosquitoes.

The cries of the children grew louder as they recognised their visitor.

'Pop, pop, pop,' they cried in unison, and Vanessa darted him a quick look; surely he wasn't the father of this group of about ten children, all of varying ages?

He grinned down at them, ruffling their hair affectionately, and Vanessa gave an almost audible sigh of relief as he held aloft a bundle of lollipops and began to distribute them. There was something about that act that bothered her, but she couldn't think what, and she had no time to dwell on it as she was now being carried further into the village amidst a sea of screaming children.

'Do you have an unlimited supply of them?' she asked as even more children began to appear from each of the tiny huts. He nodded, digging his hand deep down into his pocket.

'I wouldn't dare come visiting if I hadn't.'

Vanessa sat down on a rush mat outside one of the huts, watching Ryan. He seemed so at ease with the children, laughing and playing and chasing them. The punishment for being caught was to be tossed high in the air, and each child tried so hard to be captured, screaming with a mixture of terror and delight that dissolved into laughter once he or she was held secure again in Ryan's strong arms.

Some time later he flopped down beside her, panting

for breath. The children scattered, a few returning later
to offer green coconuts that were filled with a clear,
sweet, cool and refreshing drink. Vanessa was then
taken on a tour of the village. Pride of place was given
to a tower; it was tall and elegant and housed a giant
yam. It was at least four feet long and was suspended
by several ropes in a wooden frame. Vanessa turned to
Ryan, perplexed; she had no idea what to make of it.

'It's a trophy,' he explained. 'It represents wealth, life
and strength, rather like corn did in the ancient cultures
of America.'

Vanessa nodded and smiled her thanks to their
escort, who beamed back at her, showing the whitest
teeth she had ever seen. It was a fascinating excursion
and Vanessa left the village reluctantly, still waving her
goodbyes as she and Ryan took to the road again.

'It's getting hotter,' he said, squinting up at the sun,
which looked like a white disc in the sky. 'I could do
with a swim, could you?' he asked eagerly.

Vanessa nodded; she hated most sports, and exercise
classes left her cold, but swimming was something she
really enjoyed. She spent every lunch-hour swimming
up and down the local public pool and could now
manage between twenty and thirty lengths without
difficulty.

'Love to,' she agreed. She was wearing her swimsuit
under her shorts and T-shirt as she had expected to go
swimming at some point in the day.

Pushing their way through the trees, they were soon
back on the beach, and shrugged off their clothes with
abandon, racing towards the water. Vanessa caught
sight of the broad expanse of his bronzed back before

he dived neatly under a wave, and her stomach clenched as a butterfly of excitement fluttered inside her.

She plunged her body into the water, sinking beneath the weight of the waves in an attempt to drown the heady desire he awoke within her. Further and further they swam, Ryan's muscular arms cutting through the water, his body as sharp as a dart. Vanessa kept a steady pace at the side of him and they exchanged smiles as they swam together. Once they were both too breathless to swim any more, they floated on their backs, enjoying the sunshine.

'This is wonderful,' gasped Vanessa, unable to believe she was having so good a time and mentally promising herself a holiday the moment she got back to England. Work seemed so far away now, not real at all.

'Yet you'd prefer to see me give all this up and go back to a smoky boardroom,' he grumbled, splashing water over her face.

Vanessa spluttered. 'Most companies have a no-smoking policy now,' she threw back at him, tossing an armful of water at him in return then flipping back onto her stomach and striking out for shore.

He followed her immediately and she could hear him catching up. The race was on and Vanessa was determined to win. She put every bit of effort into each stroke and made it to the shore moments before him.

She stood waiting for him, a smile of victory on her face that began to fade when she saw that his eyes were no longer impassive as they scanned her dripping body. The wet material clung to her naturally curvaceous body and her hair had fallen loosely over her shoulders.

He moved closer to her, his eyes filled with a warm sensuality as his hands fell on her shoulders. She stiffened in resistance as he pulled her body to his. Instinctively she raised her hands as a barrier against him and pressed them against his hard, wet chest. She wanted to ward him off, to force him away, to make him keep his distance, but her defences were already weakening; part of her longed to feel his body against hers, the contrast of the strong and the weak.

He wrapped a well-muscled arm around her waist, pressing her against his hot, strong body, then his hand gripped the back of her head, holding it firmly so that she could not avoid him. The cry of protest Vanessa was about to give was lost as his lips crushed against hers. He was an expert, as she had expected—not that she was considering his technique; she was lost in a spiral of emotions.

Nothing had ever prepared her for the sheer overpowering sexual feelings that surged through her inexperienced body. A heady cocktail of desire and passion vied with the fear of the unknown, but even her fear was gradually replaced by desire as his kisses continued. She felt her knees buckle, but he held her tightly and she soaked up his strength like a sponge as she began to respond.

Her movements were tentative at first for this was unknown territory to her, but she was eager to explore, to experience the new delights that were being offered. She moved closer, enjoying the feeling of his body next to hers, the thrill of a man's touch as his hand descended over her back, drawing her ever closer to him till she could feel the whole length of his body pressed against hers.

The hardness of his body sent a shiver of anticipation trickling down her spine and her stomach clenched as a fresh series of delights raced over her. His kiss was controlled but passionate, making her feel wild and abandoned. Part of her cried out for more whilst her brain tried desperately to pull her back from the edge of the abyss she was being drawn towards.

Vanessa ignored the sensible reasoning of her brain, her body refusing to acknowledge the danger she was in. She was lost in her own sea of turmoil, her emotions spiralling so completely out of control that she was not aware that he had drawn back at first. Then she felt the icy space between them and her eyes flew to his in confusion, her breathing as ragged as his as they faced each other in a tense silence. The strength of their arousal had taken them both by total surprise and they were forced to accept the surprising knowledge that they were attracted to each other.

Ryan recovered his power of speech first.

'Maybe Robert's a better judge of women than I gave him credit for,' he mocked, viewing her with renewed interest, a sensuous grin playing on his lips.

'I find that type of remark quite offensive,' she informed him coldly, embarrassed by her body's unexpected betrayal, which she was still struggling to comprehend.

'Why offensive? I should have thought it was a compliment,' he taunted.

'Obviously living away from the civilised world has affected your judgement, Mr Searle,' she returned, her expression bland despite the turmoil that raged within her.

'You're quite wrong there; your reaction to me was quite normal. . .' he began, with a wicked grin of delight creasing his face.

'You arrogant swine!' exclaimed Vanessa in disbelief. 'I can assure you, Mr Searle...' She flexed back her shoulders in a display of strength but the action was wasted on him. He had already turned away, shrugging his broad shoulders.

He tossed carelessly back at her, 'Look, Miss Mann, I think you're overreacting to what was merely a little kiss; I'll catch you later when you've calmed down.' And, with that, he began to make his way across the beach.

For a moment Vanessa was too stunned to speak or move. A chaotic jumble of thoughts and feelings raged through her body. Firstly she couldn't understand her wild, uncharacteristic behaviour towards him and secondly she wondered if her lack of experience had made her blow the whole situation out of all proportion.

She quickly pulled herself up. She had no time to waste indulging in self-analysis; she was here to work and was determined to put the proposal back on the agenda.

'Mr Searle,' she called as she hurried after him, and he stopped immediately, taking her by surprise. She drew alongside him, a little breathless. 'Let's forget about that unfortunate incident,' she said, smiling, knowing that it was branded on her mind for ever. 'Put it down to the heat of the day,' she concluded, hoping he would be kind enough to agree.

'An unfortunate incident?' he mocked, his eyes sparkling with delight. 'The heat of the day?' he repeated in disbelief, looking at her scornfully and enjoying her discomfiture.

'I am here to work, Mr Searle, and you still haven't given me your decision,' she reminded him, trying to hide the element of defeat that she knew was present in her tone.

'Ah, well, Miss Mann, here is my decision. . .' He paused as if weighing up his answer, then said, taking her by surprise, 'I shall be returning to England with you,' and although his voice was flat his eyes held the dangerous light of controlled anger.

CHAPTER FOUR

VANESSA glanced down impatiently at her watch; the minutes seemed to be dragging. She sighed as she paced back to the foyer doors, then heard the low rumble of the aircraft's engines as it began to circle the island. She pivoted back round, picked up her overnight case and slipped her briefcase under her arm.

She'd had no contact with Ryan since he'd told her that he would be returning to England and now she suspected he'd merely said that on the spur of the moment, to disconcert her. Though she would have thought that such behaviour was completely out of character.

'Ready, Miss Mann?' His clear voice cut through the warm air, taking Vanessa by surprise. Her eyes widened still further when she looked at him. 'I have a car waiting to take us to the jetty,' he continued, his voice filled with calm authority though she could tell by the gleam of silvery light in his eyes that he knew the effect his presence was having on her.

He was leaning against the doorjamb and the transformation was total. His long, lithe body was now enclosed in a smart dark navy business suit, his immaculate white silk shirt offset by the slash of a bright-coloured tie. His hair had been trimmed considerably, the short cut drawing attention to his perfect features and the cool silver-grey of his bright eyes.

He gave her a long, penetrating look, the steel in his

eyes stinging her to the very core of her being, but she masked her turmoil well and met his gaze head-on. The pull of sexual attraction was incredibly strong; nothing could have prepared her for the impact he would make on her with his more civilised image. The depth of emotion shocked her and she momentarily closed her eyes to shut out the sight of him.

Yet she could still feel his eyes on her, the intensity of his look warning her of his displeasure. She had won a victory of sorts but she wondered now at the price she might have to pay. Working for the Knight Corporation if she succeeded in this venture seemed a dangerous prospect now. The thought of working alongside Ryan was daunting.

'You are ready, Miss Mann?' he asked again, a flicker of annoyance in his eyes as he extended his arm to take her case. Vanessa stiffened, her mouth tight and compressed. She handed him the case and swept past him, getting in the car without even acknowledging his presence. He followed her and Vanessa froze as he slid in next to her, his thigh briefly brushing against hers and sending a series of excited shivers through her body.

'So you have been successful, achieved your aim; after ten years in the wilderness I'm now returning home,' he drawled, flicking his long, tapered fingers over his muscular thigh to remove some specks of dust.

'The prodigal son returns,' replied Vanessa, forcing a casualness into her voice that she did not feel.

'Do you think they will have killed the fatted calf for me?' he taunted.

'Do they know you're coming?'

'*No*,' he replied emphatically, then added in a softer

tone that did not hide the bitterness he felt, 'I thought I'd surprise them.'

'I'm sure you will,' Vanessa said, her voice heavy with sarcasm.

'I fail to see what you have to complain about. You have been successful; you had to get me or my shares and you have me,' he teased lightly.

'It wasn't a personal vendetta; I was merely doing my job,' she retorted briskly, any triumph she might have felt in her success having faded completely.

'I was rather hoping it was.' His voice had taken on a seductive, honeyed warmth. 'I liked the idea that you might be taking a personal interest in me.' He lowered his head to see the effect he was having on her and Vanessa struggled to keep her face totally expressionless.

'I hardly think that's likely, Mr Searle; I like to keep all my relationships on a business level,' she told him firmly, hating to admit that she had never had the time or inclination to develop any personal friendships— with males or females.

'All work and no play makes Jack a dull boy, and I know that beneath that hard shell you surround yourself with there lies a very passionate woman craving for some love and attention.'

'Thank you, Dr Freud,' Vanessa snapped. He wasn't the first man to come along and suggest that he would melt her heart of stone. The arrogance of men never ceased to amaze her, but this was one who made her wonder if she had armour thick enough to keep him out.

'There's no need to be so touchy,' he complained, laughing at her caustic remark.

'I'm not being touchy; I really just fail to see what my personal life has to do with you.' And she turned her head to look out of the window, signalling that the conversation was at an end.

'I see; it's all right for you to poke your nose into my private life, even to the extent of compiling a dossier and totally disrupting my life, but yours is sacrosanct. That hardly seems fair.'

'Fair? Fair?' Vanessa flung at him as she swung back round to face him. 'Life is one big joke to you, isn't it? Even this,' she said, flicking her hand to the view beyond the window. 'Leaving here and coming back to England, it's just all a laugh to you.' She hated him, hated his smug, joky manner, his casual approach to the strong attraction she felt for him. He made her nervous, awoke feelings within her that frightened her.

'I face life as it is and I might as well do it with a smile instead of a frown,' he retorted, his jaw stiff. 'Do you think I want to leave here, leave these kind people?' he grated. 'To join a society filled with people like you?' he snarled, his mouth curling upwards in contempt.

'People like me? You don't even know me. You know nothing of me—nothing!' she almost yelled back, hating the implied criticism of her.

'Oh, but I do, Miss Mann. I've met lots of women like you in my time—cold-hearted bitches who only turn on the passion and charm when they think they can get something out of it,' he tossed at her, his face a picture of contempt and anger, his words like a hard slap on Vanessa's face.

'Your low opinion of women is only matched by my opinion of you. . .' she said, and, warming to the subject, intended to go on to tell Mr Searle exactly what she thought of him, but at that moment the car came to an abrupt halt, having reached the jetty.

The next few moments were taken up with boarding and Vanessa didn't have a chance to continue, but she stored her feelings away deep inside her, with the skill of a true professional, where they festered, eating away at her, adding to the pain that was already hidden there.

She heard him sigh as the plane rose and cast him a covert glance from the magazine she was reading. She saw the flicker of disappointment in his steely eyes as he gazed out of the window at the clear blue sea and the tiny jewel of an island that he was leaving behind.

'Sorry to say goodbye?' Vanessa said softly, suddenly hating herself for robbing him of this paradise that she knew he loved.

'Naturally,' he said, his eyes never leaving the window. 'I have been very happy there,' he said, his voice sad and wistful.

'You can come back once the problem has been sorted out,' she pointed out.

'No, that's highly unlikely. I may come on holiday to see old friends but. . .' She could hear the pain in his voice and her guilt strengthened.

'Surely it would have been easier to sell your shares and remain here? You didn't have to come back,' she argued.

'Suddenly feeling bad about your role in this whole affair?' he challenged, sensing that she did feel bad about it.

'Why should I? You had a choice and you have decided to return; I feel no responsibility for that.' She faltered, unsure if she had done the right thing, but reminded herself that her whole career was at stake here. She had merely carried out her client's wishes—successfully too—so why did she feel so bad? It didn't make sense.

'Sell my shares, just like that?' he said scornfully, grimacing at her naïvety.

'They were offering you a good price; it was a more than generous offer,' she told him, and saw his hands tighten, his knuckles turning white, as he struggled to control himself.

'Thirty pieces of silver; that's what Robert was offering—thirty dirty pieces of silver.' His voice was harsh and guttural and his head spun round to face her, his hurt and anger blazing in his eyes. She shrank back from his look of fury and he leant over her, his hard, muscular body almost on top of her. She trembled at his proximity but his highly emotional state prevented him from being aware of it. He was consumed by his anger and she was the only one around whom he could take it out on.

'He knew I wouldn't sell—couldn't sell. The bastard set you up and you, poor fool, thought you'd achieved something,' he snarled at her, his eyes sparking. He ran an icy finger down her face. 'You had better wise up if you're thinking of joining the big boys.' He laughed cruelly as he sank back in his chair, snapping his seat belt around him and closing his eyes. The sudden outbreak of emotion had left him exhausted but he had awoken every nerve in Vanessa's body and there were questions she wanted answering now.

'Why was I sent here, then, if he knew you wouldn't sell?' probed Vanessa, hating the thought that Robert had used her and that she had been too blind to see it.

'As I have already explained to you, Miss Mann, you have. . .' he paused as his silvery eyes flickered open and trailed over her body '. . .certain extra qualifications that our family lawyer, a balding ageing man, does not possess,' he drawled, a smile of triumph curling his mouth.

'Are you seriously suggesting that I was merely chosen because I'm a woman?' she asked incredulously, her heart beating out a rapid tattoo as his heated gaze remained on her.

'Not because you are a woman but because you are an extremely attractive one—and not just physically, you understand.' He smiled as he inclined his head in mock admiration of her looks, and Vanessa felt colour flood into her face. 'Robert knows I want more than that. . . No, you have a quick mind, intelligence and a sharp wit that I think could be amusing under the right circumstances,' he concluded with a smile that was brilliant, warm and above all totally genuine, and it was the sincerity that took Vanessa by surprise.

'I don't believe it,' she said, shaking her head. The idea was totally preposterous in this day and age, and yet a niggling doubt flickered to life in the back of her mind.

'Believe me, Miss Mann. Robert would do anything to get my shares—use anyone. But don't feel so bad— he must have offered you something for your trouble?' he enquired, his dark winged brows rising in curiosity as he awaited her reply.

'A permanent position at the company,' she confessed a little sheepishly, dropping her lids over her eyes because she couldn't bear to see the accusation in his.

'Well done; it's quite an honour to be employed at Knight's,' he told her, his tone sincere, and she looked up in surprise. 'I mean it; it's quite a coup.'

'I can't possibly accept the position now,' Vanessa said glumly.

'I don't see why not; you have brought back the prodigal son and that was the deal, wasn't it?' he said, his voice soft, his expression one of gentle understanding.

'That's not the point; Robert used me—' she began, but Ryan cut in, his expression instantly stern and his voice as sharp as a razor.

'Then use him,' he snapped. 'Take up the position. If you don't then you're merely cutting off your nose to spite your face,' he argued, but Vanessa wasn't sure.

'How can I?' she pleaded. 'I'd look a fool, be a laughing stock; I want to be employed because of my brains, my ability, not the shape of my legs.' Anger was swiftly replacing her disappointment.

'You succeeded; I'm going to take up my position on the board again. That's what you were employed to achieve and you achieved it.' There was a trace of bitterness in his tone that did not go unnoticed. 'Besides, you'll be in a better position for revenge if you're in the company,' he added with a mischievous grin.

'Is that what you're planning on doing?' Vanessa asked, suddenly wondering about his motives for returning.

'The plans I have for the Knight Corporation have been under way for some time.' He gave her a chilling smile that did nothing to reassure her. 'This is a golden opportunity for you; it would be senseless not to take it up. Just accept the fact that you're attractive and that sometimes it will work to your advantage but most times it won't,' he said cynically, and Vanessa was forced to acknowledge the wisdom of his argument.

'Maybe you're right. I'll think about it,' she said noncommittally.

'Now let's get down to business,' Ryan announced, straightening himself up and producing a slim briefcase from underneath his seat. 'These are the last papers I have about the company; I assume you have some more up-to-date information?' he said, opening his case, ready for work.

For a moment Vanessa was too numb to move. Ryan had managed to switch from beach bum to businessman with such ease, it was unnerving.

'I have a few papers but I fail to see what use they would be to you,' she told him, pulling her own brief-case up onto her knees.

'Obviously I'm a bit rusty so I need to brush up; there have no doubt been some major changes in the past few years,' he admitted ruefully.

'Are you conversant with computer technology?' Vanessa queried, suddenly aware of how much he had missed out on.

'A little,' he confessed a little sheepishly. 'I suppose that's essential now, isn't it?' he added, with a lazy grin which made her stomach flip.

'I have a laptop with me; I could run through a few basics with you though I'm no expert,' Vanessa offered. She felt it was the least she could do for him.

'That's great,' he said, leaning a little closer as Vanessa flicked on her machine. She turned to face him and found they were too close for comfort. An inner voice warned her that she was about to tread on thin ice but she didn't draw back. She could smell the deep, rich scent of his musky aftershave; it was intoxicating and she breathed deeply, taking in the very essence of the man.

She knew she was blushing—she could feel the heat burning her cheeks—and she could see the amusement in his eyes. He was teasing her yet his face held a tenderness she did not expect and the effect it had on her frightened her. She swallowed nervously but she was enjoying basking in the warmth of his smile.

'Why do you never wear your hair loose?' he asked, his tone gently critical, and he raised his hand, stroking down the sleek line of her hair, taking her by surprise.

'It's unprofessional,' she said crisply, hating the way her stomach flipped at the merest of touches.

'I think it looks better loose,' he drawled seductively, moving closer till she could feel his warm breath caressing her ear, making her heart thud against her chest.

'I thought that you wanted to work,' she chastised him with a trembling smile, though she was enjoying his teasing manner.

'I do; I'm waiting for you to start,' he mocked encouragingly, and Vanessa was not sure whether or not she was overreacting to him. She flushed again at the thought then turned her attention firmly to the job in hand. But she was acutely aware of him the whole time; his body was like a heated magnet, drawing her to him, and several times Vanessa had to pull herself back as their bodies got too close.

'You learn fast,' she commented after he had successfully completed quite a complex program. 'Your finger dexterity is remarkable considering you haven't used a computer that often,' she added as she watched his hands speed over the keyboard with a familiarity that was normally born of experience.

He stopped abruptly, looking at her with a quizzical expression that gradually faded into a gentle smile.

'I can type—I suppose that's why,' he offered by way of an explanation.

'Yes, that would explain your ease with the keyboard, but you've picked everything up as if you were used to computers.'

'That's hardly likely since I've been on a virtual desert island for the last ten years,' he joked, but there was a sudden wariness in his voice that perturbed Vanessa, though she couldn't quite put her finger on what was wrong.

'We should be landing soon; our connecting flight to Hong Kong will just give us enough time for lunch,' she informed him as she saw the flashing light above their heads warning them to belt up.

'And I know just the place,' enthused Ryan with a smile. But Vanessa shook her head.

'I'm afraid not. I work to a very tight schedule; we won't have time to leave the airport complex as the connecting flight will be within, hopefully, half an hour,' Vanessa explained, though she would have loved to see Hong Kong.

'You work too hard; you should take things a bit easier,' he told her with a frown.

'I enjoy work; I have little time for. . .'

'Enjoying yourself.'

'I do enjoy myself; I enjoy work,' she snapped. She

knew her whole life was work but she had never considered it a problem till she had met Ryan Searle.

'You should learn to relax a bit more; it would do you good,' he told her with a ring of authority in his tone that she found irksome.

'We are all different, Mr Searle. You may be able to afford a more laid-back attitude to life, I unfortunately do not have the security of a family to fall back on,' she ground out, furious at his cavalier attitude to work.

'You have no family, then?' he asked quickly, picking up on her words, and Vanessa panicked.

'Not as such,' she replied evasively. 'Certainly not as rich as yours, that's for sure,' she hit out, believing attack to be the best form of defence.

'Strange, isn't it, that whilst you have obviously worked hard to escape your family I gave up work to escape mine? There's a certain irony there, don't you think?' He gave a dry, humourless laugh but Vanessa's sense of humour had evaporated completely. He might have changed his outward appearance, she thought grimly, but he was basically a spoilt, rich wastrel who didn't appreciate what hard work was. Her normally soft mouth firmed to a thin line at the thought and it did not go unnoticed.

'Touched a raw nerve, have I?' he asked with amazing accuracy, interrupting her thoughts.

'Not at all,' she lied unconvincingly, dismissing the idea with a look of contempt.

'I think I did, but then again you're very touchy. Is it me or PMT?' he asked, his grin broadening at the look of horror Vanessa cast him.

'Isn't that typical?' she retorted, summoning up all her strength. 'And any woman who doesn't fall at your feet in a state of sheer ecstasy is frigid, no doubt,' she jeered.

'See, you are touchy, always on the defensive,' he complained good-humouredly.

'I'm not on the defensive, nor am I suffering from PMT. . .' Vanessa began.

'Good God, I dread to think what you're like when you are; you must be a she-devil!' He laughed at the very thought but Vanessa just glared at him.

'How come you consider yourself such an expert on women's problems anyway?' she scoffed as the plane bumped onto the runway.

'Simple—I read a lot, and virtually every woman who came to the hotel brought magazines, all of which contained articles on a whole array of women's problems,' he explained with a wicked grin.

'That hardly makes you an expert, merely well read,' retorted Vanessa, struggling with her case.

'Take this as an example,' he said, taking the case from her hand. 'Am I being patronising in carrying your case or just good-mannered? There was a fascinating article in the October issue of *Femme* that discussed this very problem.' His laughter was barely contained now and a low rumble could be heard in his throat.

Vanessa threw him a look of anger and marched off the plane. She could hear his explosion of laughter and it rang in her ears, infuriating her. Not wanting him to catch up with her, she expertly vanished into the heaving crowds. She went to one of the cafés, where she ate only half of the vegetarian meal she'd ordered before pushing it to one side, then sat sipping an iced tea.

The humidity was awful, despite the fans that whirled

unceasingly overhead. She had taken off her jacket and wrapped it around the back of her chair but the heat was still unbearable, fraying her taut nerves even further. The arrival of Ryan, still smiling, only compounded her frustration.

'Hi,' he said casually, dropping down beside her, apparently untouched by the heat, although he had loosened his tie; she could see a few stray hairs peeping out of his shirt... 'You didn't eat much,' he commented, nodding in the direction of her plate.

'I wasn't hungry—it's the heat,' she explained quickly before he began to quote from yet another article. Knowing him, he might decide she was on a diet or had anorexia.

'That's understandable,' he agreed as he attracted the waiter's attention. 'Do you want anything else?'

'No, I'm fine, thanks,' she said a little too hastily and his eyebrows rose as he sighed audibly. 'Honestly, I'm fine,' she added quickly. She was too hot to carry on fighting; she didn't have the energy for it.

'That's all right; no problem,' he said, dismissing her with a short wave of his hand.

'Look, we are just two very different people, with different ideals, values, views on life. I doubt we'd agree on anything if we talked till we were a hundred, so let's just agree to differ, shall we?' She offered the olive branch, hoping it would be accepted.

'Are we?' he asked, watching her reaction closely.

'Are we what?' she countered impatiently. All she had wanted was his polite agreement; she should have known that was an impossibility.

'So different. I somehow get the feeling we're not,' he said pensively, taking his drink from the waiter with a smile. 'I bet if you'd just loosen up a bit we could have a lot of fun together,' he concluded.

'I've no desire to have *fun* with you,' she retorted, her tone containing all the disgust she felt at the suggestion.

'Haven't you?' he asked, his voice suddenly dropping an octave and becoming deeper, a dark, slumberous warmth coating his words as he leant closer, resting his elbows on the table, till his head nearly touched hers. Vanessa knew he was toying with her, seeing how she would react to him, and she stiffened, refusing to allow herself to react. 'Relax, Vanessa,' he purred, his smoky voice sending a shiver of anticipation down her spine, her name suddenly sounding special, magical. No one had ever spoken her name in that way.

'I am re. . .' She faltered as she lifted her head and realised how dangerously close they were. She could feel his warm breath on her already heated face, see the dark orbs of his cool, sharp eyes, which were now taking on a sensual glow.

He moved his face closer and Vanessa closed her eyes as his lips briefly touched hers, a gentle caress as soft as the wings of a butterfly. She opened her eyes as he drew back, hating herself for the surge of disappointment that had struck her when she'd realised that he was not going to deepen the kiss.

She flushed in annoyance when she saw the smug smirk that curved his mouth and the superior gleam of triumph that sparkled in the depths of his eyes as he rested back in his chair, studying her with undisguised amusement.

'I see you as a real challenge, Vanessa,' he commented as he sipped his drink. 'Such a confusing combination—all ice and fire—but no doubt one day that ice barrier will melt. I hope I'm around to see it,' he concluded with a wry smile.

'If it ever happens then I hope you're around too, Mr Searle, then you could drown in the resulting flood,' she snapped.

'Drowning in the sea of your passion sounds wonderful to me,' he said, grinning, but Vanessa was already on her feet, glaring at him with all the pent-up confused feelings that were raging inside her.

'I find your attitude to women quite offensive,' she stormed, unable to cope with his humorous approach to life—especially sex. Her own experience had been disastrous.

'You don't know my attitude to women,' he complained, unaware of the distress he was causing her.

'I know your attitude to me,' she countered forcefully, her sea-green eyes sparking with renewed indignation.

'I'm sexually attracted to you,' he laughed. 'That's a compliment,' he added, as if he thought she needed that reassurance, and he smiled at her with a wicked grin that was full of sexual promise.

'I can do without compliments like that,' Vanessa said frostily, her body a stiff pole of outrage as she viewed him with distaste despite the excitement that pulsed through her body.

'Really? That's interesting,' he told her, his voice low and pensive, and he looked at her thoughtfully, his scrutiny unnerving her.

'Is it?' she tossed at him carelessly, already sensing the cracks forming on the thin ice she was treading on.

'Yes.' He sighed, before continuing, 'Where does this

hang-up originate from? What dark, secret past made you this way?' His voice lacked the joky tone it had had before now; there was a serious element to his question.

'I haven't got a past,' she threw at him. She had run away from all that and had no intention of ever going back. 'I look only to the future,' she added confidently.

'That's what I did, Vanessa,' he replied softly, 'but the past has a nasty way of catching up with you.'

'Mine won't,' she said emphatically. There was no way her family would ever find her—or would even want to, she thought grimly.

'Don't be too sure; ten years on a remote island and the past still found me,' he said, his voice now sounding like the voice of doom, a terrible portent of events to come, and Vanessa felt an icy shiver trickle down her spine. She did not want to pursue the conversation any further; the truth of his words frightened her. She knew that if she allowed the memory of her past to reach out and touch her again she risked destroying all she had worked so hard to achieve.

The blood drained from her face as a vivid image of her home flashed through her mind: the squalid, dirty room, with the pall of cheap cigarettes heavy in the air, and her parents, both the worse for drink, slumped amid the filth, unaware of their daughter's needs.

'Vanessa, Vanessa.' Ryan was at her side, drawing her towards him, and she rested against him, basking in his strength and power. 'Are you sick? Come on, sit back down; it's this bloody heat.'

Vanessa allowed herself to be seated, the image of her past fading with Ryan's reassuring words.

'I'm all right now,' she told him, taking a few deep breaths.

'It must be the heat,' he told her as he watched her closely, his sharp, perceptive eyes scanning her face.

'Yes—yes, it must,' agreed Vanessa, giving him a weak smile and nodding in agreement, but when she looked up she could tell that he didn't believe her though he smiled in response. There was something in his eyes—a cold, icy flicker—that warned her to be on her guard.

Vanessa closed her eyes to shut out his image. From the moment she had accepted this job she'd had a feeling of foreboding, and nothing that had happened since had done anything to change it. There was no way she was going to work at the Knight Corporation; some inner sense warned her that if she did her life would be changed for ever.

CHAPTER FIVE

THE lift doors slid silently back and Ryan stepped inside. Vanessa froze. She had been expecting that they would meet sooner or later, but as she had managed to avoid him for the last three weeks her fear of ever having to face him again had begun to diminish.

'Good morning, Miss Mann. How are you?' he said crisply as the lift doors shut.

'Very well, thank you, Mr Searle,' she replied equally formally, raising the sheaf of papers she was carrying up in front of herself as a flimsy barrier against him.

'I'm glad you decided to join the team; I'm sure you're going to be an asset to the company,' he said coolly, his eyes briefly flicking over her, causing her stomach to clench into a tight knot.

'I'll certainly do my best, Mr Searle,' she replied, her face expressionless despite the turmoil that raged within her.

'The work Robert assigned you—are you making any headway with it? He has given you a special task, hasn't he?' he asked, his tone casual, but Vanessa started; her job was supposed to be top secret. 'It's quite all right; I've been welcomed back into the fold and I am aware of your role, though naturally only Robert and myself are fully aware of the details,' he added with a conspiratorial air.

'It will be a long process; whoever is purchasing the Knight shares is at pains to cover his tracks. Some have been purchased through brokers and the Exchange, but unfortunately the majority have been purchased from ex-employees. All employees used to be allowed shares every year—like a bonus scheme.'

'Yes, I know; it was my idea to give staff a share in the profits,' he told her with pleasure.

'Yes, well, they add up to a lot of shares, and they are being bought via a personal approach,' she explained. 'This ensures the Knight Corporation never even has a chance to buy.'

'That's interesting. But who would have access to the employee list—surely only personnel?' he said thoughtfully.

'Maybe, but most of the people approached are the ones who have been made redundant, so I doubt it involves anyone still in the company,' she replied as she nervously plucked at her papers, trying to avoid the intensity of his gaze.

'There were thousands made redundant,' Ryan admitted grimly, his sharp eyes narrowing. 'You'll never be able to track them all down.'

'Most are still in the area and some have been quite willing to talk to me. They sold their shares long since through the banks.' She couldn't disguise the excitement in her voice now and she smiled brightly, but before she could continue Ryan cut in, his voice flat and cold.

'Some haven't, though?' he asked sharply.

'Not everyone had to; some of the redundancy payments were generous, depending on the circumstances. I hope to see a man this afternoon who has received a letter asking him to sell his shares to an unknown third party. . .'

'And he is reluctant to do that?' Ryan probed, ignoring the fact that the lift had come to a halt.

'On the contrary, the thought of the Knight Corporation being in difficulty delights him; he now wants our offer to be greater than the one already made,' she said hurriedly as she went to leave the lift, but Ryan's strong arm reached out and stopped her. His fingers wrapped around her upper arm, making her feel momentarily weak and vulnerable. She swallowed nervously.

'So what are you going to do?' he snapped.

'Meet him, of course. If he can throw any light on who is buying the shares any price will be worth paying,' she said, and shrugged her arm free from his grip, partly in annoyance and partly because of the havoc that his touch was creating within her.

'He won't be able to tell you anything if they are being bought through a third party,' he argued logically, but there was a noticeable sharpness to his tone.

'He might. If this man is so eager to buy he might reveal his identity if asked especially and if the seller is sympathetic to his ideas,' she threw back, pleased that she had covered every angle.

'When is this meeting taking place?' he asked, stepping from the lift and letting the doors close behind him.

'Later on this morning, actually.'

'And where does he live?'

'Westside Estate.'

'Forget it!' snapped Ryan, his expression grim and forbidding.

'I beg your pardon?' said Vanessa, quite indignant. She had worked hard to arrange this meeting and she certainly wasn't going to be dictated to and dissuaded from going through with it now.

'I said forget it; there's no way you're going to any private meeting there,' he ground out, and his eyes, nose, mouth—every feature on his tightly controlled face—radiated anger.

Her skin chilled as a map of goose-bumps covered her arms. 'I can assure you, Mr Searle, I've every intention of keeping this appointment, with or without your approval,' she retorted briskly, spinning away. She hated this type of confrontation but was used to standing up for herself.

He did not allow her to escape. He gripped her tightly by the shoulders and spun her back round to face him. They stood glaring at each other, Vanessa furious at his high-handed attitude and determined to stand her ground.

'You're not going to that estate—it's dangerous; it's a no-go area. You've no idea what you're letting yourself in for...' He was going to continue but Vanessa was not going to let him.

'The Westside Estate holds no fears for me,' she replied confidently, thinking that it was not far removed from where she had grown up herself.

'Oh, I see, so because you're not afraid that means you won't be mugged or raped,' he snapped back sarcastically, his eyes bright with barely controlled anger.

'I'll take the necessary sensible precautions but I *am* going to that meeting. It's my first major breakthrough and I'm not about to let it slip through my fingers,' she retorted, facing him.

The strength of her determination made him pause for a minute and he viewed her thoughtfully.

'Then I'll come with you,' he finally announced with a smile, his anger disappearing as quickly as it had been aroused.

Vanessa lifted her chin a little higher, looking aloof and cool, and shook her head resolutely.

'I'm afraid that's out of the question; I need this man's trust and I'm hardly going to get that if you're there,' she explained, and, sensing that her words would meet with disapproval, stepped back a little.

'Why not?' he snapped.

'He is selling his shares to the highest bidder to get some money together; the man is obviously desperate. And why? Because this company made him redundant. You're hardly likely to be at the top of his Christmas card list, are you?' she retorted, flexing her shoulders in a show of assertiveness.

'I didn't make him redundant; I wasn't even here then,' he countered, his anger fully stoked now, and for once he looked about to lose control of himself.

'Oh, no, you were living the life of Riley on a wonderful island in the Pacific; that's really going to make him feel you care,' she threw at him.

'I do care; if I'd been here those job losses would have been quite unnecessary,' he said vehemently, his voice sounding strangled, full of pain.

'But you weren't here, were you?' she snapped. 'You were too busy enjoying yourself. You care? That's too much like hard work,' she scoffed bitterly. 'The only thing you've ever cared about is yourself.'

'That's not true!' he declared, his voice sharp, angry,

and he looked away with eyes that shone with an irritation that was matched by the tightening of his jaw.

'Isn't it?' Vanessa mocked. 'Well, I'll pass on your kind regards to Mr Haven just to see his reaction, shall I?'

His head spun round so fast, his eyes blazing, that for a moment Vanessa thought she had overstepped the mark.

'John Haven? Is it John Haven you're going to see?' he demanded excitedly.

'Yes. . .' Vanessa faltered. 'I think that's his first name; I'd have to check, though.'

'Then check and get back to me; I want to know,' he growled, before marching off, leaving Vanessa staring after him. She knew the man's name was John without even checking and a feeling of unease crept through her body.

Her worst fears were confirmed. Once Ryan had been told it was indeed John Haven he insisted on accompanying her.

'John and I go way back,' he revealed as he tried to make himself comfortable in Vanessa's small car. She frowned as he shuffled about, grunting irritably—she disliked this forced intimacy as much as he did. 'We should have gone in my car,' he complained as he struggled to move the seat back to give himself more leg room.

'Hardly,' said Vanessa disdainfully, checking the road before pulling out into the busy traffic. 'A car like yours would attract too much attention; besides, there's no guarantee it would even still be there when we came back to it—car thefts are rife on that estate,' she informed him, aware that her hand touched his thigh each time she changed gear.

'And what makes your car immune?' he taunted.

'It's not, but if you were out for a joyride you'd hardly choose a car like this,' she said good-humouredly. 'The salesman said when I bought it that it was a real woman's car.' Vanessa gave a hoot of laughter as she recalled the incident.

'What did he mean by that?' asked Ryan, shifting uncomfortably, his movements restricted because of his size.

'Well, other than that it's not big enough for great hulks like you, I think he meant it was unable to go from nought to thirty in ten seconds,' she said crisply.

'Essential in any car,' said Ryan, smiling.

'Especially if you're a bank robber,' agreed Vanessa, and she returned his smile. For a brief moment they were enjoying each other's company.

'You need a bigger car, though,' mused Ryan, his eyes taking a slow, calculated look at the length of Vanessa's legs. She flicked him a sharp glance but his only response was a wicked smile that made her feel weak inside.

'I'm quite happy with the car I have, thank you,' she told him frostily, but his grin merely widened even further. 'It's cheap to insure and economical to run.'

'Is that a silly hint that we're not paying you enough?' he teased as he began to flick through her collection of tapes.

'No, but I've recently become the owner of an apartment in Granby Row and I'm afraid the mortgage takes up most of my spare cash,' she told him, the pride in her voice tangible.

'Granby Row—very posh!' He laughed. 'I see you like Curtis Stigers.' There was a note of rare approval in his tone as he slipped the tape in. Vanessa mumbled a reply; she hardly wanted to listen to romantic ballads with Ryan Searle; it was far too intimate... She cast him a covert glance but he had rested back in his seat and closed his eyes to allow the gentle rhythm of the music to wash over him.

'I think this is it,' Vanessa said a few minutes later as she drew the car to a halt, and leant across him to peer out of the window. The house was set back from the road, there was a small garden and a grey gate swung to and fro at the bottom of a paved path.

'Number twenty-eight?'

'That's right,' Vanessa said, taking a deep breath. She glanced round. The street was quiet—almost too quiet. Graffiti adorned any spare piece of wall and litter blew up and down the pot-hole-ridden road. Some of the houses were boarded up, adding to the sense of decay.

'There's no place like home,' Ryan said grimly as he climbed from the car and scanned the area.

'Just count yourself lucky you don't have to live here,' Vanessa snapped. This was familiar territory to her, and she was experiencing an unwelcome trip down memory lane.

'How can they live like this?' Ryan asked, partly angry, partly bewildered.

'They have no choice; most estates are pretty much the same, some slightly better than others,' Vanessa said, locking her car and mentally rejoicing at the fact that she had escaped yet pitying all those who remained, trapped by unhappy circumstances and poverty.

'Yes, but there's no need for that,' Ryan said, pointing to a huge graffiti-covered wall that dominated the bleak landscape. He frowned at the sight of the dull and peeling paint.

'Perhaps not,' Vanessa said wearily, shrugging. She had heard all the middle-class arguments before and for a time, at university, she had actually agreed with them. Now, however, coming back to the environment of her childhood, she wasn't so sure of their validity.

'Well, that's just wanton vandalism,' Ryan said dismissively, his eyes narrowing on Vanessa when she didn't reply. 'You do agree, don't you?' he asked, his tone already incredulous as he sensed that she didn't.

'Does it matter whether I agree or not?' she asked evasively, hating his superior attitude towards a lifestyle he knew nothing about, and she wondered how his attitude towards her might change if he found out the truth about her.

'It's vandalism,' he repeated as they walked up the path to the house.

'More than likely the result of boredom,' Vanessa declared.

'That's no excuse,' he snapped as he rapped impatiently on the door.

'It's not meant to be an excuse, just an explanation. What did you do when you were bored? Did Nanny take you down to the pool for a swim?' she taunted.

His face paled with anger at her words but before he could reply the door opened slightly, a chain preventing them from entering.

'I don't believe it,' a small, grey-haired man said, directing a beaming smile at Ryan. 'It's young Mr Searle—Ryan?' He laughed, releasing the chain and drawing the door further back. 'Come in, come in; it's a pleasure to see you. Sorry about the chain. It's the wife—she's a bit nervous. Come on in and sit down. I'll put on the kettle.'

Vanessa sat and listened in surprise whilst John and Ryan discussed old times. This was a side of Ryan she had never seen before; far from the snob she'd imagined him to be, he seemed quite at home in the humble surroundings, even washing up the dirty crockery in the tiny kitchen after they'd had a cup of coffee.

Finally, however, once they were all sitting down in the living room, he got down to business. 'Now, John,' he said, suddenly serious. 'Are you selling your shares?' He winked at him as he spoke, teasing the old man, who responded with a wink of his own. 'Perhaps I should explain. This is Miss Mann; Robert has employed her to discover who is buying up Knight shares,' he told him, and they exchanged a knowing look which Vanessa failed to comprehend.

'I'm looking for a high price for mine,' John Haven said grumpily.

'Why are you selling, John?' asked Ryan, his voice soft and concerned, and he leant forward to encourage the old man to confide in him.

'I need the money. My wife's nerves are shattered; we've been burgled three times in the last year—not that we have much; it's been the telly and the video every time,' he explained sadly. 'There are some new bungalows being built on the old market site; it's close to town and the bus routes and it's away from here,' he finished grimly.

'Have you any idea who's buying them?' asked Vanessa. This was the information they had come for and she didn't want to be sidetracked, even if Ryan wanted to indulge the old man.

'No, I don't, but whoever he is he has more money than sense.' He smiled almost cruelly.

'What do you mean?' Vanessa asked, wondering how much this man really knew.

'That company is going down the tubes; I saw it coming. It will take a miracle to pull it back,' he said, sucking on his unlit pipe for comfort.

'Miracles do happen,' Ryan said consolingly as he got to his feet. 'Now can I buy those shares?' he asked.

It took just a few minutes to sign the papers and soon Ryan and Vanessa were back in the car.

'What on earth did you do that for?' Vanessa asked in amazement.

'Do what?'

'Pay five times more than those shares were worth,' she said, totally bewildered.

'How else would he be able to afford a bungalow? Besides, I owe him far more than that,' he said quietly, but refused to divulge any further details.

'Still, he wasn't much use to our inquiry, was he?' Vanessa said. She hated failure; she worked hard always to achieve results. 'It's been a waste of a day,' she complained.

'Not entirely. I caught up with an old friend, we have prevented the mystery buyer getting some more shares and meals are still being served at the French bistro on Cannon Street,' he drawled, a triumphant ring to his voice.

'I fail to see the relevance of the French bistro,' Vanessa snapped, already guessing what he had in mind.

'I thought we could go there for lunch,' he said. 'I'm starving,' he tacked on, to add weight to his idea.

'I'll drop you there if you like but I'm afraid I've work to do,' she told him, keeping her eyes firmly on the road as she could tell he was laughing at her.

'I don't want to eat alone; besides, I want to talk to you, get to know you better,' he teased.

'If you don't want to eat alone I suggest you try the staff canteen—' Vanessa began, but he cut in, his voice flat and hard.

'You never use the staff canteen,' he admonished her.

'I had no idea it was compulsory,' she retorted, hating the way she was always on the defensive with him.

'It's not, but I'm curious to know why you never use it,' he probed gently, and Vanessa sank her teeth into her bottom lip.

'I normally bring a packed lunch,' she said breezily. 'I eat in my office—is that all right with you?' she asked sharply, trying to avoid the cool look he was giving her that told her he had seen through her pretence.

'Why do you spend your life avoiding people, Vanessa?' he asked, his voice so gentle, so full of concern that for a moment she hesitated, almost tempted to confide in him, but she knew she could not afford that luxury.

'I go to the office to work, not to develop a social life,' she told him scornfully, but the jibe did not perturb him in the least.

'I don't think you have one,' he said.

'Have what?'

'A social life. I think you scurry off home and hide

away in your new Granby Row apartment, safe and secure.'

He was mocking her and it hurt. The truth of his words was like a slap across the face; she swallowed the painful, constricting lump in her throat and blinked away the searing pinheads that pricked against the back of her eyes. She had been happy—no, not happy, but content with her life before she had met Ryan Searle. He seemed determined to turn it upside down, she mused.

'It's true, isn't it?' he asked when she refused to answer. 'Come on, Vanessa, where's your sharp tongue? Aren't you going to recite a list of exciting pursuits you undertake after work, give me the names of all your many friends?' he continued to tease, only wanting a response, not realising how much he was hurting her.

She remained silent as she manoeuvred the car into the car park at the French bistro, then turned to face him. 'Your lunch awaits,' she said, keeping her voice as bland as her expression, but her eyes had softened with unshed tears and they looked like soft pools of sea-green water, deep and fathomless but so inviting.

Ryan looked at her then turned away, discomfited by the evidence of her pain, which he knew he had caused.

'I've upset you, haven't I?'

'Not really, no.'

'Yes, I have.'

'Yes, all right, you have. Since I met you, Mr Searle, you have done nothing but poke fun at me. I've worked damn hard to achieve what I have and I've never had time to develop a social life. I left home at sixteen, entered university at eighteen, qualified, and have spent the last five years trying to find a secure position. I don't want your pity or your respect; what I want is for you to just leave me alone.'

'Can I say something?'

'Yes,' snapped Vanessa, knowing her words had fallen on deaf ears.

'I'm sorry.'

The words hung between them, the very air suddenly seeming rarefied. Unconsciously they were both holding their breath as they gazed at each other. She knew he meant it—she could tell, and slowly a smile crept over her face.

'Let me make amends—come to lunch?' he pleaded. 'My treat,' he added as an extra incentive, and all of a sudden it seemed to Vanessa churlish not to accept the olive branch that was being offered.

'Yes, thanks; that would be nice,' she agreed, realising that she was hungry.

'Great; let's go.' He gave her a smile—a bright, dazzling smile that held a fatal charm which she knew she was not immune to.

Inside the bistro the muted lighting added to the atmosphere of intimacy, and the tiny corner table they were shown to looked too cosy, too private, Vanessa thought as she slid into her seat.

'This is nice,' Ryan commented as he joined her, picking up a menu, and Vanessa smiled in response but she was too on edge to relax. She was too aware of him—of his strength, of his calm resilience—and his constant sense of fun disturbed her because it made her so acutely aware of how much was lacking in her own life.

'Why did you leave home at sixteen?' he asked

suddenly, catching her off guard, and Vanessa stiffened. She was about to trot out her familiar lie about living with an aunt, but there was something in his sharp, glittering eyes that warned her he would not be fooled. She felt trapped; she wanted to bury her past, not have it dragged up by him.

'I wanted to,' she said, picking up her menu and scanning it in order to avoid his eyes. He reached out and took it from her, forcing her to face him. She confronted him with equal candour but her strength soon failed her and she dropped her gaze.

'Why, at such an early age?' he probed, and Vanessa swallowed the nauseous feeling that churned in her stomach.

'It didn't seem it at the time; I was ready to leave. I had ambitions so I went; it's that simple.' She forced a smile to her lips.

'Nothing is that simple,' he told her, still keeping his eyes fixed firmly on her. 'But let's drop it, shall we? I want to enjoy this meal, not stir up a hornets' nest.' His expression was full of understanding but his eyes shone with interest, warning her that it was a conversation he would return to.

As they ate their meal Vanessa was amazed to discover how much common ground they shared; for example they had a mutual interest in wildlife documentaries, loved the same authors. She was quite relaxed, was even beginning to enjoy herself, and she had just ordered coffee when a shadow fell across the table. She looked up immediately.

'Ryan?' a voice asked seductively, a trace of doubt in the tone. 'It is, isn't it? Ryan!' the female exclaimed in delight, and a smile swept over Ryan's face too as he leapt to his feet.

'Vicky! How marvellous. You're looking well.' He planted an affectionate kiss on her proffered cheek and Vanessa felt her stomach clench. This woman was the epitome of class; every inch of her was made up to perfection, from the understated simple checked suit which Vanessa instantly knew was Chanel to the tiny black bag bearing a Gucci clasp.

'I heard a whisper you were back,' she purred, flicking her hair back to reveal a beautifully made up face.

'And you've been looking for me ever since,' Ryan teased. His eyes softened as he spoke and the tenderness that Vanessa saw in their expression gave rise to a sharp stab of pain, though she didn't care to question why.

'I admit I've been round a few old haunts.' She gave a girlish giggle. 'I've found you now,' she crooned.

'You always were determined; you always get what you want,' he said, his criticism softened by his smile.

She pouted as she drew nearer, a sulky look on her face. 'Not everything, Ryan,' she cooed.

'Come on, Vicky, your broken heart soon mended. Six months later. . .' His eyebrows rose quizzically.

'It didn't last, Ryan—you spoilt me for anyone else,' she said, her eyes bright with a flare of sexual interest.

Vanessa watched the pantomime being played out in front of her. She had taken an instant dislike to Vicky and hated the way Ryan was behaving; he was actually enjoying the woman's fawning attention.

'Oh, Vicky,' he said, shaking his head in disbelief. 'I somehow doubt that very much.'

'It's true!' she exclaimed. 'Come on, let's have a

DOUBLE YOUR ACTION PLAY...

"ROLL A DOUBLE"

Peel off label & place inside

CLAIM 4 BOOKS PLUS A FREE GIFT

ABSOLUTELY FREE!

NO RISK, NO OBLIGATION TO BUY...NOW OR EVER!

GUARANTEED

PLAY "ROLL A DOUBLE" AND GET FIVE FREE GIFTS!

HERE'S HOW TO PLAY:

1. Peel off label from front cover. Place it in space provided at right. With a coin, carefully scratch off the silver dice. Then check the claim chart to see what we have for you - FREE BOOKS and a gift - ALL YOURS! ALL FREE!

2. Send back this card and you'll receive specially selected Mills & Boon Presents™ novels. These books have a cover price of £2.10 each, but they are yours to keep absolutely free.

3. There's no catch. You're under no obligation to buy anything. We charge nothing for your first shipment. And you don't have to make any minimum number of purchases - not even one!

4. The fact is thousands of readers enjoy receiving books by mail from the Reader Service™, at least a month before they're available in the shops. They like the convenience of home delivery, and there is no extra charge for postage and packing.

5. We hope that after receiving your free books you'll want to remain a subscriber. But the choice is yours - to continue or cancel, anytime at all! So why not take us up on our invitation with no risk of any kind. You'll be glad you did!

You'll look a million dollars when you wear this lovely necklace! Its silvertone chain is a generous 18" long, and the exquisite floating heart completes this lovely gift.

"ROLL A DOUBLE!"

PLACE LABEL HERE

SCRATCH HERE

SEE CLAIM CHART BELOW

P7BI

YES! I have placed my label from the front cover into the space provided above and scratched off the silver dice. Please rush me the free books and gift for which I qualify. I understand that I am under no obligation to purchase any books, as explained on the back and on the opposite page. I am over 18 years of age.

BLOCK CAPITALS PLEASE

Ms / Mrs / Miss / Mr _____

Address _____

_____

Postcode _____

CLAIM CHART

 4 FREE BOOKS PLUS FREE FLOATING HEART NECKLACE

 3 FREE BOOKS

 2 FREE BOOKS

CLAIM NO. 37-829

drink,' she added, linking her arm through his and drawing him away from the table. Ryan looked over his shoulder, forcing Vicky to acknowledge Vanessa—something she obviously didn't want to do. 'Oh, I had no idea you had company,' she lied, her eyes narrowing on Vanessa before making a swift critical appraisal of her.

Vanessa lifted her chin. She knew she was equally well groomed but she lacked the innate confidence that this woman had. She forced a cool smile to her lips and inclined her head but remained silent. She was curious to know how Ryan would introduce her.

'Vicky, you must meet Vanessa, my future wife,' he said casually, giving Vanessa a brilliant smile that lit up his whole face.

CHAPTER SIX

VANESSA stared at Ryan and opened her mouth to protest but he sank down beside her, wrapping his fingers around her wrist in a punitive grip, drawing her hand to his mouth and planting a kiss on her palm. His actions silenced her as her stomach flipped and her heart skipped a beat.

'Should I offer my congratulations?' Vicky asked, her tone sharper now and her features bearing the strain of this revelation. 'Or is it a little premature?' she asked spitefully.

'No, this time I intend to make it up the aisle.' He laughed, but Vicky's mouth thinned to a grim line at his words.

'I hope you know what you're taking on, Vanessa,' she said. 'Has she met the family yet?' she asked, flicking Vanessa a glance that expressed her belief that she wouldn't be up to the mark. Vanessa stiffened at the implied criticism, and she knew that was ridiculous as she wasn't going to marry Ryan.

'I'm sure they will all adore her, like me,' Ryan replied with a smile. 'Let's crack open a bottle of bubbly and you can join us in a drink,' he suggested lightly, and Vanessa felt her cheeks burn. This had gone far enough. She sprang to her feet, glaring at Ryan, and pulled herself free.

'Is this a lovers' tiff?' laughed Vicky, enjoying the display of open hostility. 'Well, make sure you keep the ring, darling; I did.' Then she cast a speculative look at Vanessa's naked finger. 'Oh, dear, no ring yet,' she said in mock sympathy.

'I've commissioned something special,' Ryan snapped. 'We'd best go; I'd forgotten Vanessa had a headache. Perhaps another time, Vicky,' he said, slipping his arm around Vanessa's waist and gripping her tightly, and despite the horrendous circumstances Vanessa felt her stomach flip at the feel of his strong arm curled around her.

'Surely you're having an engagement party at the Manor? Ours was a huge affair.' Vicky tried to force a note of gaiety into her voice but the stinging bitterness still came through.

'Not as large as that. Vanessa is a quieter person, doesn't like a lot of fuss,' Ryan explained, applying a little pressure to Vanessa's side to make her move. 'Look, we must be going. Lovely to have seen you, Vicky; do keep in touch.'

The women exchanged a forced smile, then, before Vanessa could speak, she was bundled quite firmly from the bistro. Ryan did not release his grip immediately and Vanessa no longer welcomed his touch. She pulled away from him as soon as they were outside.

'What the hell do you think you're playing at?' she stormed, ignoring the large drops of rain that had begun to fall.

'It seemed like a good idea,' Ryan began sheepishly, but Vanessa didn't even bother to wait for explanations, she was so angry. How dare he use her to protect himself? The man was despicable.

She marched over to the car park, every inch of her body betraying her pent-up frustration and annoyance.

Ryan didn't follow at first and Vanessa used those moments to her advantage. She climbed into her car and wasted no time in starting the engine. She flicked on the windscreen wipers just as the heavens opened and the rain began to lash down.

She could just about hear Ryan call her name over the roar of the engine as she pressed down hard on the accelerator. Glancing into her rear-view mirror, she saw him waving frantically, but she paid him no heed; he could walk back to the office for all she cared, though knowing him he'd probably take the afternoon off, she thought grimly as she swung back onto the main road.

Vanessa went into her office, shutting the door with a bang. She had never felt so angry in all her life. She sank into her chair, pulled open a desk drawer and guiltily looked at the bar of chocolate that was in there. She slammed the drawer shut again; she was not going to seek comfort in chocolate so she decided to use work as a panacea for her temper.

She had barely got started when the door was flung open with such force that it crashed against the wall, the icy blast of air sending her papers into disarray. Vanessa's head shot up and there stood Ryan. He was wet through, his hair was dripping, and he pushed it back from his face as another raindrop fell onto his nose. His eyes were blazing and his unspoken anger emanated from every inch of his body. He hadn't been wearing a coat and his suit shone with the soaking it had taken.

For a moment the child in Vanessa shrank back, but she checked herself immediately and sprang to her feet, welcoming the confrontation. There were a few things she wanted to tell Ryan Searle.

'If you wouldn't mind closing the door, Mr Searle,' she said in a frosty tone, hoping to gain control, but Ryan's normal iron restraint had gone. He lifted his foot and kicked the door shut without even taking his eyes off Vanessa. His action only increased Vanessa's dislike for him even further; she had been raised in a violent home and displays of overt aggression did not impress her.

'How dare you leave me stranded in a car park in the pouring rain?' he growled, the dark orbs of his eyes fixed on her with cold intent.

'Leave you in a car park?' she echoed in disbelief. 'How thoughtless of me to leave my poor fiancé,' she threw back, her jaw aching as she spat the words out through clenched teeth.

'Oh, so that's your problem!' he said, as if the truth of the matter had suddenly dawned. 'I never took you for the type who'd want revenge.'

'Oh, I'm the petty one, am I?' she mocked. 'That's rich. I never wanted to go for lunch in the first place and you only wanted to so you wouldn't have to work,' she asserted, glaring at him but glad of the table that was still separating them.

'Actually I went to lunch because one, I was hungry and two, fool that I was, I thought it might be fun,' he told her, his voice flat and hard, but she ignored the veiled compliment; she only had room for anger.

'Fun! That's your byword, isn't it? I suppose it was fun to pass me off as your future wife,' she snapped, leaning on the table for support as she faced him, her eyes molten pools of heated rage.

'Well, lady, it's probably as close as you'll ever get to marriage,' he said, suddenly taking Vanessa by surprise by shrugging off his jacket and shaking a series of raindrops over her office.

'Thank God for small mercies. Marriage holds no attraction for me and certainly not to a man like you.' She hurled the words at him, hoping that they stung, but his reaction was too swift for her to discern what effect they'd had.

'A man like me?' he ground out, leaning across the desk, his manner threatening. 'What do you know about men, Little Miss Prim?' he scoffed.

'I know plenty about the male species, all of it rotten, and your behaviour has done nothing to improve my opinion,' she told him coldly.

'My behaviour...?' He sounded surprised but Vanessa wasn't going to let him continue; she hadn't finished yet.

'You are bone-idle, you have no respect for your family, no idea of commitment. You have wasted your life and think you can use women for your own ends,' she declared, hating the man. She felt it was a fair appraisal of him and expelled her breath as her temper evaporated.

'So that's your considered opinion, is it?' His voice was now dangerously quiet, low and menacing, and he moved away from the desk and slowly made his way around the table. Vanessa watched his approach, her eyes dilating as he drew near. 'You hold me in very low esteem, don't you?' he asked, and his voice held an unmistakable trace of anger strangely mixed with another emotion that Vanessa couldn't recognise.

She felt her mouth go dry and could only nod in

silent agreement. She swallowed quickly, forcing herself to find her voice; it was her only barrier against him.

'I think this conversation is at an end, Mr Searle,' she told him, and her voice sounded rather high-pitched even to her ears, and she knew she had taken a step back as he advanced closer.

'So do I, Miss Mann,' he drawled. 'I've always believed that actions speak louder than words.' His voice had dropped an octave and become strangely hypnotic, seductive and warm, but that only increased Vanessa's fears. She could feel her heart thumping against her chest, drumming in her ears, and her stomach curled into a tight knot as she read the message that was shining in his glittering eyes.

'Ryan...' His name escaped from her lips in a whisper but he moved even closer, taking her word as an invitation, and Vanessa was suddenly overwhelmed by an urgency deep within her that seemed to be taking over all logic and sense, her fear quickly changing to expectation. The tension in his face disappeared and all the harsh angles seemed to soften, giving him an aspect that was an odd combination of gentleness and strength.

Vanessa instinctively licked her lips, completely unaware of her action, her mouth softly parting in a soft invitation. She knew he was going to kiss her, and ever since he had kissed her on the beach she had longed for it to happen again. She wanted to feel him, taste him, absorb his strength and power, and yet there was that familiar element of fear that still niggled in the darkest recesses of her mind.

He drew her up against him, burying his face deep into her warm, sweet-smelling hair, pulling at the grips till they fell tinkling to the floor. He ran his fingers through her tresses, nuzzled down to her ear and planted a gentle kiss on her lobe. Vanessa felt her knees buckle and clung to him for support. He wrapped his hand around her neck, pulling her close and fastening his mouth on hers.

At first his kiss was hungry and demanding, with a passion that took Vanessa by surprise, but she responded eagerly. Then his kiss deepened and Vanessa felt even weaker as the warmth spread throughout her body, awakening in her all the locked-away feelings that she had kept guard over for so many years.

His arms tightened around her and her own clasped his back, smoothed over his shoulder. She could feel the taut strength of them under his shirt and the sensation of his rippling muscles aroused her even further, despite the warning bells that were beginning to ring at the back of her mind.

His kisses became gentler, persuasive and soft. Vanessa melted into his arms and they became one, their bodies slowly meshing together in a non-musical ballet that seemed to have its own natural choreography. She was aware of every inch of him; every fibre of his body seemed linked to hers and she did not want to break the embrace. She felt so safe, so wanted that she sank beneath the waves of contentment that were washing over her.

Lost in their own world, they failed to hear the sharp rap on the door and they broke away, startled, when they heard Robert's voice.

'Vicky Standford wasn't wrong, then,' Robert said as they looked at him.

Vanessa's face was red with self-consciousness. She lifted a well-manicured hand to her head as she attempted to scoop her mass of hair back up; she needed to do something, she felt so agitated.

'I'll tell you all about it, Bobby,' Ryan said, knowing Robert hated his childish name for him, then he turned and kissed his fingertips before placing them gently on Vanessa's lips. 'Catch you later,' he said huskily, and Vanessa nodded mutely in reply, unable to comprehend what was happening to her or the situation she was in.

She made her way to the Ladies, where she rearranged her hair with quick dexterity and reapplied a fine coating of lipstick. She gazed at her reflection and a flicker of a frown creased her forehead. She looked the same—Vanessa Mann, the cool-headed executive—yet there was a light in her eyes that hadn't been there before, a glow to her face that had not been contrived with make-up. Vanessa stared, turning her face from side to side to look at every angle. There was a change—she could see it, sense it—but what really worried her was that she couldn't tell whether that change was so obvious that other people might see it.

She made her way quickly back to her office, closed the door and threw herself into her afternoon's work. Yet try as she might thoughts of Ryan seeped back into her mind, invaded her senses. She could still feel his lips on hers, taste him; his aftershave seemed to permeate her nostrils, flooding her senses with the very essence of the man.

She was relieved when the clock finally reached five and she could escape. The last thing she wanted was to face Ryan again—at least not till she had made some sort of sense of the whole crazy situation.

* * *

She breathed in deeply as she entered her flat and closed the door on the day's troubles. She loved coming home; this was her first real home, the one she had always dreamt about. It was clean and fresh, the bed neatly made, a pile of fluffy soft towels in the bathroom, and the fridge was full of select food. It was her sanctuary and she loved it.

She made her way into the cosy lounge and selected a favourite CD. The gentle sounds filled the room. Then she quickly prepared a simple salad and placed a foil-wrapped breast of chicken in the oven, setting the timer before she went to shower.

Afterwards she put on a pair of grey marl leggings, a matching baggy shirt and a pair of thick socks. As she made her way back to the kitchen, she shook her hair out, letting it fall in thick, heavy locks over her shoulders. As usual she ate her meal in front of the television: though she hated to admit it, she was addicted to even the worst of soaps.

She was so engrossed in her programme that at first she didn't hear her intercom buzz; she normally ignored it anyway, since she had no friends or family to visit her. Tonight, however, the caller was insistent. She got up and pressed her button.

'Yes?' She waited for the caller to speak and was shocked to hear Ryan's voice.

'Hi. Can I come up?' he drawled, as if he were a constant visitor.

'What for?' asked Vanessa cautiously, her heart already thumping at the mere sound of his voice. This was her special place, her home, and she wasn't sure she wanted anyone invading it—least of all Ryan Searle.

'I want to talk.'

'Can't it wait till tomorrow?'

'No.'

'Why not?'

'For God's sake, Vanessa,' he snapped. 'We need to talk.'

She didn't reply but simply pressed the control button that opened the main door. Then she quickly plumped up the cushions, took her dirty plate away, snapped off the television and reset her CD. No one had ever visited her home before and she wanted to ensure it looked perfect.

She opened the door and waited for a fraction of a second before saying, 'Come in.' She flicked her hair from her shoulders as she caught him looking at it.

'Very nice,' Ryan commented as he stepped over the threshold, and Vanessa wondered where the compliment was directed, then noticed that he was looking at the array of prints that covered the length of the hall. 'Where did you get these?' he asked, stepping closer to take a better look. 'They are quite wonderful.' His tone held a rare note of approval.

'You'll think me an awful vandal,' she confessed, 'but I've taken them from old books.'

'How very clever—a real home-maker.' He grinned at her and her heart soared at such an unexpected compliment.

'Come through. Do you want a drink—tea, coffee? I don't have any alcohol in,' she said sheepishly, suddenly realising that even if she didn't drink she should have some in for guests. Not that she had any guests, she quickly reminded herself, feeling a momentary disappointment.

'Tea will be fine. I never drink and drive,' he said,

sitting down, and Vanessa suddenly felt very self-conscious.

He sensed her awkwardness and smiled.

'I'll just put the kettle on,' she said, and smiled back, unable to stop herself from reacting to him yet glad to put some distance between them.

'It's very nice here. There's a sports complex nearby too, isn't there?' he called to her as she busied herself in the kitchen.

'Yes—two squash courts, a gym and a swimming pool,' she confirmed. 'Not that I use them,' she added quickly.

'Why not?' he probed gently. 'You're a great swimmer.'

'I don't want to get involved,' she said vaguely, putting the tray down on the coffee-table. 'Help yourself to biscuits,' she said as she sat down, unaware that he was watching her closely.

'Get involved with what?' he asked.

'Oh, I don't know,' she said, shrugging expressively. 'People, I suppose. I mean, if you got to know them and you all lived in the same place there would be invites to dinners, parties. . .'

'And you wouldn't want all that.'

'No,' she replied emphatically, shaking her head, her hair making a cloud of soft colour around her face. 'Not at all.'

'Quite the recluse, aren't you?' he teased, helping himself to an unhealthy amount of sugar.

'I enjoy my own company. I know that's considered a crime these days but I actually like the tranquillity of being by myself,' she argued, sipping her tea and hoping he wouldn't find any flaws in what she was telling him but knowing he would.

'Surely you get lonely sometimes?'

'No.' She hesitated. 'Not really.'

'Liar.'

'I don't,' she declared hotly. 'I like my own space.'

'What a disgusting phrase.' He screwed up his nose to express his disapproval and Vanessa smiled.

'It's true,' she protested.

'Don't try to fool me,' he said, putting down his cup and fixing his eagle eyes on her. 'You're running away as fast as your little legs can carry you. You're hiding away in here because what's out there frightens you. But what is it out there that poses such a threat to you?' he asked, his voice calm and composed although there was a hint of steel in his tone, a hardness that she heard quite clearly.

'I don't know why you work in an office when it's obvious you really want to be an analyst,' Vanessa said, cleverly fielding his question with her flippancy.

But he was not so easily swayed and asked again, his voice a little more forceful, 'What is it, Vanessa? Who or what frightens you?'

'Nothing,' she snapped crossly, getting to her feet in agitation.

'Then why do you live like a nun in cloisters?' he asked, a smile softening his otherwise serious face.

'Because I want to,' she spat at him. 'Now, what do you want? I presume this isn't a social call.'

'Then you presume wrong. Why else should I visit you?'

'How did you get my address?' she asked, suddenly

troubled. She had been so surprised by his arrival that she had forgotten to ask him before.

'Personnel were very co-operative,' he said casually, still smiling, but he did not fool Vanessa. She knew he had a mind as sharp as a knife.

'No doubt they were,' she said scathingly. 'But what exactly do you want?' she persisted. He was disturbing her, intruding into her private life, and his questions were far too penetrating. He had the ability to reach into all those dark places where she had hidden away her emotions all those years ago.

'What are you offering?' he said suggestively, a hungry look gleaming in his eyes, his voice low and husky.

Vanessa felt a hint of colour rise to her cheeks. 'What are you doing here?' she demanded, ignoring his easy banter. She couldn't play these sexual games that he found so easy.

'Visiting.'

'Come on,' Vanessa snapped, her patience at an end. She hated the fact that he was joking when part of her longed for him to be telling the truth. It would have been so nice if he had just come to pay a social call.

'It's about our engagement,' he confessed, avoiding her gaze and concentrating on pouring himself another cup of tea.

'Pardon?'

'Our engagement,' he offered with a sheepish grin, and there was something in his tone that troubled Vanessa.

'We're not engaged,' she reminded him forcefully, her teeth clenched.

'No, not yet,' he admitted, grinning from ear to ear, but Vanessa merely stared at him, stony-faced.

'Not yet?' she repeated warily. She sat down, trying to bank down the frisson of excitement that raced down her spine. She knew he was joking, that he couldn't possibly be serious, and yet for one fleeting moment the thought of being engaged to Ryan seemed wonderfully appealing.

'That's what I want to discuss,' he told her, settling back on the couch and stretching his legs out in front of him, totally relaxed and at home.

'What?' Vanessa hated his calm composure; she knew he was toying with her and it infuriated her.

'Now don't get mad,' he told her, raising his hand in supplication. 'Just wait—'

'What on earth are you talking about?' Vanessa interrupted, her eyes angry, burning pools of outrage as she glared at him.

He sighed, letting his shoulders slump in exaggerated defeat.

'Robert saw us together. Vicky had phoned to ask him if our engagement was real and when he came to ask us—well, you know the rest,' he finished lamely.

'And you told him it was complete nonsense, of course,' Vanessa said doubtfully, twisting her hair round her fingers in agitation.

'Of course.'

'Thank God for that,' she sighed, but her relief was tinged with a slight sense of disappointment—though she did not question herself too deeply as to why that should be so.

'I told him there was no way we could be engaged till you'd met Grandmother Searle.'

'You what?'

'My grandmother—she is the matriarch of the family,' he told her, his voice serious, and a dark shadow scurried through his eyes at the mention of her. 'She'd expect to meet you before we got engaged,' he concluded, his voice grim and his mouth thinning to a bitter line.

'But we're not getting engaged,' protested Vanessa, a cold feeling of dread beginning to form inside her as she noted the change in him. He was no longer his usual self.

'Not yet.'

'Will you stop saying "not yet"? We are not nor are we ever going to be engaged.'

'Why not?'

'Why not?' she repeated, her tone full of scorn. 'Are you crazy?' she asked, jumping to her feet.

'Crazy for you,' he drawled as he got up and took her in his arms, and despite everything Vanessa felt her stomach flip at his touch.

'Stop it,' she shouted, pulling herself free, her arms still burning from the contact with him. 'What are you playing at?'

'OK, I confess. I want you to be my fiancée.'

'No.'

'Just for a time.'

'No.'

'Please.'

'Why?'

'I should have married Vicky Standford; she was my fiancée. I. . .' He hesitated, a little embarrassed.

'Jilted her!' Vanessa threw at him in disgust. 'The act doesn't bother you but the words stick in your throat,' she added scornfully, and the vehemence with which she spoke caused him to look away to avoid her accusing eyes.

'I thought I loved her... I think I did,' he said pensively.

'What a unique way of showing it,' she scoffed, telling herself that this only confirmed what type of man he was.

His head swung back round, his eyes bright with a mixture of pain and anger. 'Vanessa,' he said, his voice flat and hurt, 'will you never give me the benefit of the doubt?' There was a plea in his voice that made her soften a little. 'I wouldn't ask you if I wasn't desperate.'

'Thank you,' she snapped.

'Sorry, but you know what I mean.' He grinned, knowing she hadn't really taken offence. 'I need your help.'

'Why?'

'Lots of reasons.'

'Which are?' She sat back down, waiting for his explanation, and he sank onto the couch, ready to explain.

'One, I want to make sure that Vicky doesn't imagine I'm available.'

Vanessa threw him a look of disgust. She couldn't believe this; she certainly wasn't going to be part of this type of deceit.

'Two—and this will probably appeal to you—I'm pretty sure that whoever is buying up the shares is part of the company,' he told her, knowing the impact his words would make. He sat back to await her reaction.

'I thought as much myself,' she said, now sitting on the edge of her seat.

'I thought you did; you were coming quite close when you tracked down John Haven,' he said with a winning smile, a rare note of approval in his tone.

'Yes, it's a pity that turned out to be a dead end, but I fail to see how pretending we're engaged will help.'

'I want people to see me head over heels in love—you too. That way they'll be put off their guard and therefore liable to make mistakes,' he told her, obviously pleased with himself.

'I see, but couldn't we just be a couple?' she asked. The implications of a pretend engagement were too serious to contemplate.

'Don't be so unromantic,' Ryan complained, with a laugh. 'This is supposed to be a whirlwind romance.'

Vanessa grunted doubtfully and looked at him with distrust. She picked up the tray and took it out to the kitchen. She needed to think.

'You'll do it, won't you?' he called out to her.

'I don't know,' she said as she came back in. 'I can't act,' she confessed, doubting his scheme would work.

'You don't have to,' he said, coming over to her, a wicked smile curling his mouth suggestively, and he planted a gentle kiss on her mouth.

'Now there's one part of our courtship we don't have to work on,' he drawled, still holding her in his arms.

'I'm not sure.'

Another quick kiss weakened Vanessa's resolve still further but she was not about to complain.

'This is crazy.'

He kissed her again, more passionately this time, and Vanessa moved closer to him, enjoying the feel of him next to her.

'Ryan,' she protested weakly as he wrapped his hand

around her neck, holding it so that her head could not move, and he kissed her again, and she responded with equal enjoyment.

'Please,' he murmured. 'It will be—'

'Don't you dare say fun,' she said, drawing back to glare at him.

'Come on, Nessie, loosen up.'

'If I agree—and it's a big if—I want to be kept fully informed of all developments,' she said firmly, trying to ignore the effect that his proximity was having on her.

'Naturally,' he agreed, his smile warming her very soul.

'Well, you obviously kept some facts from me,' she complained.

'Not really,' he said a little awkwardly. 'Anyway, I won't any more. Lovers shouldn't have any secrets,' he mocked, and Vanessa thought about all the secrets she carried, would always carry, and how the burden seemed to be growing heavier with the years, not lighter.

He moved closer, their bodies fusing a little too intimately together, and Vanessa felt the familiar twist of panic in her stomach. Kisses were one thing but the thought of anything else terrified her.

'We're engaged in name only,' she reminded him as he buried his face in her hair, his warm breath caressing her neck and making her stomach curl in anticipation.

'You smell wonderful,' he murmured.

'It's medical shampoo for lice,' she told him.

'Careful, Vanessa, you're developing a sense of humour,' he mocked. 'It smells of peaches; I love peaches.' He inhaled deeply.

'Then go home and open a tin and leave me in peace,'

she told him as he teased her hair through his firm fingers. Vanessa hated this, hated the way he made her feel. It was dangerous; she knew he was a womaniser, that he cared for no one, but despite knowing all that she was still not immune to his fatal charm.

'You know you don't mean that,' he crooned, nibbling at her earlobe, and Vanessa moaned in delight.

'I do,' she told him, trying to be firm, but it was pointless; her body was intent on betrayal.

'You're a terrible liar,' he teased, his arm descending, and he slipped his hand under her loose top and Vanessa gave a start as she felt his hard, warm hand on the naked flesh of her back.

'Go,' she told him firmly, moving away. This was going too far, too fast.

'Oh,' he complained, the heat and hunger in his eyes frightening her. 'Do I have to?'

'Yes,' Vanessa told him, escorting him firmly to the door.

He turned as he stepped over the threshold. 'I suppose you have something really classy to wear for tomorrow night?' he said casually.

'Tomorrow night?'

'We're meeting Grandmother Searle at the Savoy.'

'You're joking!' exclaimed Vanessa, her heart stopping for a second as she realised just what she was taking on.

'For once I'm not.' He gave her a wry smile then planted a quick kiss on her lips. 'See you,' he said, then added, 'Missing you already, darling,' before bursting into laughter.

Vanessa closed the door on his laughter and went back into her flat. It seemed strangely quiet, though the musky aroma of Ryan's aftershave, which still hung in the air, was strangely reassuring. She sat down, rested her face in her hands and shook her head. This was the craziest thing she had ever done in her life; there was something about Ryan Searle that made her behave completely out of character. She should have refused; she was playing a dangerous game, she admitted to herself, and if she wasn't careful she was going to get hurt—very hurt.

CHAPTER SEVEN

VANESSA cocooned herself safely inside her office the next morning. She wasn't sure if anyone knew about her and Ryan yet, but once the news hit the grapevine she knew it would spread as quickly as wildfire, fanned by the gossips.

A sharp rap on the door mid-morning made her jump, and she smiled in surprise as Robert popped his head round.

'A minute, Miss Mann?' His tone was polite but held an unmistakable ring of authority that made Vanessa instantly jump to her feet. She had Robert to thank for this post, and once this farce was over with Ryan she hoped to remain there, didn't she? she told herself.

'Of course. Do come in,' she said politely. She sensed he felt uncomfortable; a damp gleam of perspiration had already broken out on his forehead.

'Miss Mann—that sounds a little official now we're to be related.' He coughed uneasily at the admission.

'Then Vanessa, please,' she said, indicating a chair.

'Vanessa,' he began, 'I'm sorry to have to say this but, believe me, I'm only thinking of you. Ryan is. . .' He faltered. 'Ryan often. . .this is difficult for me. . .' he hesitated, looking flustered.

'Then let me help you. Ryan cannot be relied on, he is a wastrel and a womaniser and to him work is a four-letter word,' Vanessa said quite calmly, though for some reason she wanted to add, But he has a great sense of fun, the sexiest smile I have ever seen and eyes that can burn you with the fire of passion or freeze you with one glacial look.

'Exactly,' he agreed, unaware where Vanessa's thoughts had travelled. 'Though it's not just that; as you know we have been down this road before, and Grandmother Searle was awfully keen on Victoria Standford. Her ideas are perhaps rather outdated, but, well, the Standford family go back a long way and family connections are important to Grandmother.'

Vanessa nodded solemnly but didn't speak; there were no words adequate to express her distaste for Robert and his snobby values at this moment.

'I hope I haven't offended you; I just wanted you to know. You see, Grandmother can be a little difficult; she and Ryan have never seen eye to eye,' he said, with a weary sigh, but there was a gleam of satisfaction in his eyes that did not go unnoticed.

'I'll bear all you've said in mind, but if you don't mind I really do have a lot of work,' Vanessa said coolly.

'How is your research coming along? Even more shares were bought up yesterday; at this rate the family will lose control,' he said, shaking his head. 'There's something rotten here,' he mumbled in disgust. 'I'm sure Ryan's involved somehow.' A dark frown furrowed his brow. 'God, if only I could pin this on him I'd have him out,' he ground out, then suddenly remembered who he was talking to. 'Though I'm sure he's not; the shares were being bought long before he returned,' he reassured her, then beat a hasty retreat.

Vanessa expelled her pent-up, angry breath. She was furious, and had no time to calm down before Ryan came sauntering in, that familiar smile curling his mouth.

'I see Cousin Bobby's been in to congratulate you,' he teased, leaning over her desk and scanning the papers she was working on.

'It was more a not too friendly warning,' she told him.

'Warning?'

'I don't think Grandmother Searle is impressed with your choice,' she told him flatly.

'The only thing you have to know about dearest Grandmama is that she despises weakness and takes pleasure in destroying those who can't stand up to her. So it's very important that you hold your ground.' A darkness had swept into his eyes and his jaw tensed as he ground his teeth together; his whole body seemed to have iced over, as if he was hiding behind a shield as he fought to gain control of his emotions.

'She sounds formidable.'

'You'll be all right; your sharp tongue is equal to hers any day.'

'Is that a compliment?' she asked with a wry smile.

'Sort of. You just make sure she doesn't put you down,' he reminded her.

'I can hold my own,' she declared, though she wasn't looking forward to having to do so. 'But as for family connections, I'm sorry but there's no blue blood in my family.' She banked down the whole rush of emotions that overwhelmed her at the mention of family ties.

'Don't worry about it; it's not for real, remember?' He laughed.

'No, no, of course,' she agreed quickly, hating the

self-pity she had allowed herself to wallow in, even if it had only been for a fleeting moment.

'So there's no problem, then, is there?'

'No, not at all,' she agreed. 'What time is dinner tonight?'

'Early, if you don't mind. She'd never admit it but Grandmother tires easily; she likes to get to bed before ten if she can, so if I pick you up about seven. . .?' His eyebrows rose in question.

'No problem; I'll finish early here, if that's OK?' she asked.

'Fine,' he replied abstractedly, his eyes focusing on her paperwork again. 'What's this?' he asked with a troubled expression as he picked up a piece of paper and began studying it.

'Just a theory I'm working on; I need a lot more figures before I can be sure,' she explained, pleased that he was taking some interest in work at last. 'The shares that are being bought—they wouldn't make any real difference to the family holding, would they?'

'What do you mean?' he questioned cautiously, as if treading on cracked ice that threatened to break beneath his feet.

'Well, like I say,' she said quickly, 'I haven't the figures but surely the family hold the majority share? So no matter how many shares were bought they would never be a real threat to the company, would they?'

'Not a threat as such, but they would certainly undermine company policy; the shareholders might not like it,' he told her, his tone calculating.

'I still think the person who's buying them must already have a large share,' she said, taking the paper from his hand and studying it again, her brow furrowing in concentration. There was something missing, she knew there was, but she just couldn't see what it was at the moment.

'Then it must be a family member. Who do you suspect—Robert? My grandmother? Me?' He laughed.

'There's no one else with shares?' she queried, sure that she was on the right lines.

'Not to my knowledge. Anyway, stop bothering about it now; no one is going to make a move till you and I relax our investigation, remember? Don't forget we're supposed to be young lovers now.' He grinned.

Vanessa didn't smile. She was still troubled. Something was staring her in the face but she just couldn't see it.

'I'll see you at seven. By the way, I've already told my secretary so the whole company should know our news by midday.' He sounded amused but Vanessa didn't respond and Ryan sensed her unease.

'What's up? You're not getting cold feet, are you?' he teased, his brows arching in a challenge that he knew she would take up immediately.

'Not at all, but how are we going to end it?'

'Easy. We just say we've changed our minds.'

'Come to our senses?' She waited to hear his agreement, secretly dreading it.

'You're a cynic, Vanessa,' he teased.

'A realist.'

'See you tonight and stop working so hard; a frown is developing on your forehead,' he said, massaging just above her eyes with a tenderness that surprised them both.

The blood began to pump through Vanessa's body at an alarming rate and she unknowingly closed her eyes to savour the moment. His fingers felt cool against her heated forehead as they pressed into her skin with firm, seductive strokes that were almost hypnotic.

'That's better.' Ryan's voice rang with approval as the frown faded from Vanessa's face. 'Now you look as beautiful as ever.'

She watched him go. Was he joking? she wondered. Did he find her beautiful? Or was it all just part of the game they were playing?

Vanessa pulled herself up. She had never indulged in such romantic fantasies before and she wasn't about to start now. It was all part of the investigation she'd been employed to undertake, nothing more, she reminded herself, a stab of disappointment searing through the armour plating she had carefully worn since she was a child.

Vanessa did a slow turn in front of the full-length mirror, taking in her appearance from every angle. Her dress was a simple sheath of the finest raw silk, dyed an aquamarine colour which held a certain iridescence as she moved. She had set her hair in rollers and had brushed it out, so that it fell in thick, soft mahogany curls over her slim shoulders, the coppery highlights a perfect foil for the green dress and her sparkling sea-green eyes.

Ryan arrived exactly at seven. By that time Vanessa was peering from her window, waiting for him, and as his car drew to a halt she hurried to the door and opened it. Her heart was thudding quickly against her chest and her breathing matched it beat for beat. He thrust a huge bouquet at her and the scent hit her.

'I hope you like red roses; they seemed appropriate.'

'Perfect,' she agreed, taking them and burying her nose in them, inhaling the heady fragrance. 'Come through. I'll just get my coat.'

'You look stunning,' he said as he followed her, his eyes burning into her back, and her heart soared at the compliment.

'You don't look so bad yourself,' she said, placing her flowers carefully down, and cast him a quick, approving look, although she avoided looking him straight in the eye, knowing that if she did her attraction for him would be obvious.

'A far cry from when we first met,' he admitted ruefully, with a tantalising grin.

'Indeed,' Vanessa agreed, picking up her coat and marvelling at how handsome he looked. His freshly washed blond hair was swept back from his face and just rested on the collar of his jet-black dinner jacket. His trousers, obviously made to measure, fitted perfectly and his black patent shoes gleamed as brightly as his sharp eyes.

He took her coat from her and helped her put it on, his natural good manners causing her stomach to clench. He was close—too close; she could smell the familiar musky scent of his aftershave and it sent her emotions into overdrive, though she managed to smile her thanks. She began to make her way to the door but he called her name, stopping her in her tracks.

'Vanessa, wait; aren't you forgetting something?' His voice was deep, dark and mysterious.

'No, I don't think so.'

'Come here.' His voice was low and quietly compelling; Vanessa looked at him warily but his seductive smile won her over and she went to his side. A tremor went through her body and a small involuntary sound escaped through her softly parted lips as she gazed in wonder at the shining diamond that glittered in its soft cushion of burgundy velvet.

'Shall I put it on?' he asked, with a momentary amusement in his eyes that vanished as their eyes met. Her skin went white then the flame of passion heated her cheeks to bright red. She trembled as he touched her but she managed to control her hand by stiffening her whole body. She gasped as the cold metal slid over her knuckle then rested perfectly on her third finger.

'It's beautiful,' she whispered, tilting her hand to and fro to see the full effect of the cluster of diamonds.

'You like it?'

'I love it. Thank you,' she said, planting an affectionate kiss on his cheek, but he caught hold of her and grasped her tightly.

'As your official fiancé I expected more,' he murmured, his voice hoarse with sudden intimacy.

His tone made her weaken, sending shivers of excitement through her body. He wrapped his arms around her in a protective clasp and drew her closer to him till her soft breasts rested on the strong expanse of his muscular chest. He was slightly taller than she, and Vanessa tilted her chin upwards, her lips curling into the beginnings of a smile. Her smile contained all the sweetness of her trust in him and for a moment he paused, but then the sensual warmth of her body overwhelmed him and his mouth sought hers, bearing down on her with searing pressure.

She melted against him; she had gained experience now and knew how he moved, how she could please him when they kissed, and she enjoyed her power and the effects her actions had on him. They drew away from each other unwillingly.

'We'll have to go,' he said apologetically, his obvious reluctance thrilling her. 'I hope you're ready for this,' he added as he put a reassuring arm around her shoulders. She had been up until that moment, but now a whole flood of doubts assailed her. She directed a frantic look at him, flicking her hair back, and it flared red in the light.

'You'll be fine. I've every confidence in you.'

'Thanks,' she said. There was something in his words and his presence that assured her that everything was going to be fine.

Vanessa frowned as she reached the car and saw the driver.

'A chauffeur.'

He grimaced as he opened her door. 'I should have warned you—Grandmother Searle still considers it the done thing.' He laughed, but Vanessa knew she was moving in a completely different league and that she was completely out of her depth. Still, it was just another role; she had been acting most of her life and had got away with it, though Ryan had come close to discovering the truth on occasion.

Vanessa insisted on two minutes to freshen herself up before she was introduced to Ryan's grandmother. She reapplied her lipstick, checked her hair, then went to meet him in the foyer. She knew he was not impressed by the ostentatious surroundings but Vanessa was drinking up the atmosphere, wallowing in it, and mentally congratulating herself at how far she had come from her humble beginnings.

'The Searle party,' Ryan informed the head waiter,

and Vanessa caught his arm, her eyes filled with sudden desperation.

'Party?' she echoed. 'I thought it was just us.'

'Just family,' he corrected her, but his reassuring smile did not put her at her ease.

'Since when has Vicky Standford been family?' she hissed as they approached the table and she caught sight of her adversary. Though why she felt they were in competition she didn't know.

'Robert's guest—he's always had a thing for her,' he said, as if unable to understand the attraction that he himself had once so strongly felt, but Vanessa didn't want to be reminded of that. He clasped her hand and gave it a squeeze, restoring her confidence with his warmth. She cast him a quick look and their eyes met, and anyone looking at them at that moment would have seen a wonderfully happy couple, obviously deeply in love.

'Grandma, I'd like you to meet Vanessa Mann, my fiancée.' The pride in his voice was evident and Vanessa marvelled at his acting ability; if she hadn't known better she would have thought he was sincere. Vanessa stretched out her hand and found it grasped in a powerful grip, the aged woman's lifeblood clearly still vital and pumping vigorously through her body.

She stared as she said respectfully, 'Good evening, Mrs Searle.'

The woman inclined her head in response, her eyes as bright as Vanessa's new ring. She wore a high-necked blouse, a dark-backed cameo fastened in the middle of the neckline just under her firm chin. It was her only piece of jewellery except for a well-worn wedding band. Vanessa noted the stick that was balanced with care on the arm of her chair but the figure before her certainly didn't look in need of any physical help. She was stiff-backed, and her vitality shone in her eyes and in the strength of her voice when she spoke.

'Sit down, Vanessa. This, as you can imagine, has come as a surprise to us all.' Her tone was flat, not welcoming, but if she felt hostile towards her she was certainly at pains to hide it.

'A pleasant one, I hope,' countered Vanessa, her voice equally controlled.

'That remains to be seen. Poor Victoria has trod the same path but as usual Ryan did not live up to expec-tations,' she told her, and Vanessa felt a momentary stab of pain for Victoria which quickly vanished when the other woman intervened.

'I may have been saved from a fate worse than death. Robert is far more reliable,' she purred, resting a possessive hand on Robert's, who beamed.

Vanessa bristled at the open attack on Ryan and jumped to his defence.

'Any expectations I have had he has always sur-passed.' She sought Ryan's face and was not disap-pointed when she saw his expression; his smile was radiant.

'Then you must have remarkably low standards, Miss Mann,' his grandmother immediately retorted. 'I've taken the trouble of ordering for all of you, including the wine,' she informed them all, giving no one a chance to disagree with her. 'But first I suppose we'd better have a toast to the happy couple,' she added reluctantly, her tone full of scorn.

Vanessa shook her head as the waiter began to fill

her glass and her action did not go unnoticed; Grandmother Searle's sharp eyes never missed a thing.

'Surely you're not refusing to drink to your own engagement?' she asked, her eyes fixed on her as if seeking out the truth, and Vanessa wondered whether or not she suspected anything.

'I don't drink,' she stated simply, and the old lady's eyebrows rose quickly in surprise, a cruel smile curling her thin, cracked lips.

'How novel. Ryan's mother loved to drink, didn't she, Ryan?' she said, turning her head and pinning her icy eyes on him. Vanessa witnessed again his iron control as he kept a firm lid on his emotions. Dark clouds passed through his eyes but he remained silent, and Vanessa knew the strain he was under though she couldn't comprehend the cause.

'Surely you remember your mother's drinking habits?' his grandmother goaded, and Vanessa jumped to his rescue.

'As it's a special occasion, I think a glass of champagne would be most apt,' she said, nodding to the waiter.

'There's no need, Vanessa,' Ryan told her, placing his warm hand across hers, making her heart race, and she smiled in response.

'Nonsense. I'm sure I'll enjoy a sip.'

'Grandmother has a lot of faults but her taste in wine is faultless,' Ryan whispered to her in a conspiratorial hiss, and Vanessa laughed.

'It's rude to whisper in company; I would have thought even your mother would have taught you that,' snapped Grandmother Searle, glaring at them both, as if she was aware that she was the butt of their laughter.

Vanessa felt Ryan's grip tighten momentarily before he smiled.

'My mother had impeccable manners, which is more than can be said for some people,' he threw back, and the criticism obviously hit home because a faint glow touched his grandmother's cheeks.

'Really, Ryan, if you can't keep a civil tongue in your head—' she began, but Ryan cut in, his eyes blazing now.

'A civil tongue in my head?' he repeated in horror. 'I think it's a bloody miracle that I even sit at the same table as you vultures,' he growled, his iron control failing him for once.

'Now, Ryan. . .' began Robert in a conciliatory tone, but Ryan was too furious to listen.

'Shut it, Robert,' he snapped. 'I don't even know why I agreed to this fiasco—'

'Enough!' Grandmother Searle interrupted, her voice low and firm and totally compelling, her eyes quickly scanning everyone at the table, daring anyone to defy her. No one did. She raised her glass. 'Long life and happiness to Ryan and Vanessa.'

'To Ryan and Vanessa,' everyone chorused, and they raised their glasses, smiled their congratulations and behaved as if nothing had happened. Vanessa was puzzled. There was something going on here, something she was not party to, and she resented the fact that Ryan had thrown her into a den of lions without her fully understanding what was going on.

After that the meal seemed to pass quite pleasantly. The atmosphere was strained but good manners prevailed and the family differences were buried under a sea of polite, banal conversation.

'Are you OK?' Ryan asked Vanessa at one point, leaning over her, his warm breath stroking her cheeks.

'Fine,' she smiled. She was as clever as he was at hiding her emotions.

'That's your third glass of champagne. Be careful—it's more lethal than it tastes,' he warned her, but it was too late—she was already feeling the effects.

'It's wonderful; bubbles burst on my tongue and race down my throat, tickling me all the way.' She laughed, her face soft and inviting, her eyes molten pools of sexual invitation when she looked at him. Her pupils had dilated to large black orbs.

'You look beautiful,' Ryan told her, raising his hand and twisting one of her soft locks around his fingers. 'Really beautiful,' he whispered.

'Thank you,' purred Vanessa, surprising herself with her flirtatious manner as she lowered her lids ever so slightly then peeped up at him from beneath her lashes. She dropped her hand to his thigh and stroked his muscle, which clenched at her touch, and she smiled wickedly, enjoying her power over him, the way his body reacted with the same abandon as her own.

'Vanessa.' Grandmother Searle's sharp voice brought her quickly back to attention and she moved ever so slightly away from Ryan, though she was still aware of the electric sexual power that surged between them. 'I was wondering about your family. I've arranged your engagement party for the twentieth and naturally your parents will wish to attend.'

Vanessa shot a look of panic at Ryan. This was getting out of control; the mention of family caused a sick, never-to-be-forgotten fear to spiral through her body.

'Vanessa and I are not keen on the idea. . .' Ryan began.

'Nonsense. This is a golden opportunity for us to show a united front—a family no longer at war, the prodigal son welcomed back along with future wife. The Press will love it and it might effectively put an end to all this speculation on the stock market,' she told him firmly, and Ryan cast a look at Vanessa, hoping she understood.

'If you'll give me your parents' address I shall write to them,' she continued, too absorbed in her own thoughts to notice how the colour had left Vanessa's cheeks. But Vicky saw her reaction.

'I have no family,' Vanessa said, her voice cold and flat.

'No family? How very odd. Surely you must have someone—a brother, sister, aunt, uncle?' persisted Grandmother Searle. She didn't like this; she liked things to be in order.

'I haven't seen my parents for years; they wouldn't be interested,' Vanessa said, trying to keep her voice calm.

'A simple invitation is merely good manners; they can refuse to come if they wish,' she insisted.

'No!' The heartfelt cry exploded from Vanessa's lips as she stood up. 'I don't want them invited; I want nothing from them,' she declared hotly, sick memories of her childhood suddenly racing into her mind from the locked closet she kept them in.

'It's all right, Vanessa, it's all right.' Ryan wrapped a protective arm round her. He was disturbed by the outburst; it was so out of character. He looked down at the empty wine flute and frowned. His grandmother did the same and gave Ryan a smile of triumph.

'They say sons choose wives like their mothers. You'd best take her home,' she said crisply, her tone dismissive and disapproving.

Ryan might have replied but Vanessa swayed dangerously at his side, taking all his attention.

'We'll take a taxi,' he said as he took Vanessa by the hand. 'Come on, we're leaving.'

Vanessa had quickly gained control, and though her heart was still thudding she managed to present a calm façade.

'Thank you for a lovely evening,' she said with a smile, before being whisked away by Ryan. His grip was tight and she cast him a wary look, wondering whether he was annoyed with her. She shrugged herself free.

'I'm not drunk,' she protested, glaring at him. 'I just didn't want this farce to go any further.'

'It has to,' he argued. 'The engagement party is heaven-sent; can't you see that?'

'My parents won't be there,' she told him emphatically through clenched teeth.

'They don't have to be, though they can't be any worse than her,' he declared. 'I owe you an apology for her behaviour. She's always like that—she's a tyrant,' he ended forcefully, his jaw hardening to a firm line.

'She has a sharp tongue but she's harmless enough,' Vanessa said, thinking about her own childhood, in which sharp words had more often than not been accompanied by an even sharper slap or the lash of a belt. She shook her head to push the dark thoughts from her head, but they were all flooding back now and she feared she was going to drown in them.

'Get me a cab quickly,' Ryan snapped at the doorman as he saw all the colour drain from Vanessa's face. A few moments later he placed her gently inside a car, barking her address to the cabbie. Normally Vanessa would have protested—she was too independent for this—but tonight she allowed him to take her bag, find her keys and generally look after her, and she actually found herself thoroughly enjoying the experience.

Once he'd settled her in her flat he brought her a hot drink and waited patiently for the colour to return to her face. Only then did he speak.

'Are your parents still alive?' he asked, his voice quiet but controlled, and Vanessa shook her head by way of a reply. 'Vanessa.' His tone was sharp and her head shot up to face him. 'Are your parents alive?' he repeated, his sharp eyes fixed on her, the silvery lights gleaming dangerously.

'I never knew my real father,' she confessed, her eyes shimmering with unshed tears. She had always imagined that things would have been different if he had been around, but deep down she knew that was a fantasy. He had not wanted the responsibility of a child so had left her mother even before she had been born.

'Then tell me about your mother.' His voice was gentler now, comforting and persuasive, but Vanessa couldn't bear to reveal how bad her past had been and he evidently understood. 'I'll tell you about mine, then; we can exchange horror stories.' He gave a hollow laugh that did not disguise his pain or bitterness. 'God, I could do with a drink.'

'I've bought a bottle of brandy,' Vanessa said, getting

to her feet and going to the kitchen; she had purchased it the other day, just in case she had a visitor, and was now very pleased that she had. Returning to the living room, she placed the bottle and a glass next to him then sat back down. He poured himself a generous measure and took a large mouthful, grimacing as it scorched his throat. Then he began, 'I hated my parents. . .'

CHAPTER EIGHT

VANESSA stared, nonplussed. Ryan hated his parents? She couldn't imagine why. He had been born with everything—social position, wealth, a loving family—what reason did he have to hate anyone? He was just spoilt, had been given too much too soon, she mused as she looked at him, but the dark shadows that were forming in the depths of his eyes told another story.

'Can you understand that—a son, an only child, hating his parents?' he asked, then shrugged and added, 'I guess not.' He sat back in his chair and swirled his brandy around in his glass, watching the amber liquid intently, lost in his thoughts.

'With some children, I can, but not you—what on earth have you got to complain about?' Her tone was sharper than she had intended but she disliked his self-pitying attitude. It seemed so out of character and it disturbed her; this was a side of Ryan she had not seen before. He was vulnerable and yet strangely that did not detract one inch from his masculinity; if anything this gentler side seemed to increase his attractiveness.

'Plenty,' he said. 'You've met dear Granny Searle,' he spat, his lips curling in disdain. 'Well, imagine her as a mother,' he said, as if the very thought was horrendous, and Vanessa nodded in understanding. She was a formidable lady.

'She ruled my father with a rod of iron. The most important thing in his life was the Knight Corporation.

His own father died of a heart attack at forty-five so he had to take full responsibility when he was only twenty—with his mother's help, naturally.'

'What a responsibility,' Vanessa remarked, but Ryan wasn't aware that she had even spoken; he was lost in his own private world of pain.

'But although he had his mother's help the company needed money—a huge influx, and fast—so a carefully arranged marriage was agreed upon. My poor sweet mother was caught in a loveless marriage that she knew she could never escape from. A different generation,' he added by way of explanation. 'Two people with nothing in common were forced to live a lie and my mother couldn't take the pressure. And my father was no help. He was weak, totally dominated by his mother, and he worked himself to death. We rarely saw him, and when we did he was always lost in a haze of cigar smoke and alcohol.'

'You hate two people merely because they were weak?' Vanessa asked, shocked. It hardly seemed fair, but for a moment something niggled at the back of her mind. . .

'No, not for being weak; that's rather sad and feeble. But they used me. All of them used me.' The words spilled out in a tortured groan.

'How?'

'The only thing they all had a common interest in was me. To Grandmother Searle, Mother and Father I was simply a commodity to be bartered with,' he told her bitterly. 'True, I had everything money could buy, but never once did anyone show me love. Every toy I was bought, every holiday I took wasn't for me; the adults were just playing power games. They fought over me like dogs with a bone.'

'That must have been hard,' said Vanessa. She could well understand the pain of not being loved or wanted. For her that cut was deeper than the physical pain she had often borne, for the pain of being unloved lasted for ever.

'Uncle Brett, Robert's father and my father's younger brother, was driving the car in the accident that killed them both. Grandmother has never forgiven Robert for that, though God knows he's done everything he can to please her.'

'It must have been hard for her, losing her two sons,' Vanessa said softly. She hadn't particularly liked the woman but she could appreciate the pain and loss she must have felt.

'Of course it was,' snarled Ryan in disgust. 'As they had both controlled the company, now their wives did, and she hated that.' He tossed the rest of his brandy back and helped himself to some more.

'Robert's mother was soon paid off,' he went on. She signed the shares over to Robert, took a huge settlement, packed her bags and went, never to be seen again.' He grimaced at the memory. 'So that was one down, one to go, but my mother didn't have Karen's confidence; she didn't know how to start a new life. Her marriage hadn't been particularly happy but it was the only role she knew how to play,' he told her, the sadness in his tone alerting Vanessa to the fact that there were more details to come.

Her heart was melting now as the full story of his miserable childhood came to light. She could identify with his loneliness and pain; it was a shared experience despite their different circumstances.

'So what happened to your mother?' she asked softly. She was intrigued by his family history and by the fact that he was revealing so much of himself to her; she knew she was seeing a part of him that he rarely, if ever, showed to anyone.

'I'll never forgive myself for that,' he said, shaking his head and closing his eyes to shut out the bitter memories that crowded into his mind. 'She committed suicide.'

'Suicide?' repeated Vanessa, a cold chill sweeping over her. It wasn't possible. Her death had been accidental—she remembered the newspaper reports at the time.

'But it was more like murder,' he growled. 'She'd do anything for control, always wanting power,' he said, and slumped down in his chair, mumbling half to himself.

Vanessa was losing the thread of the conversation. 'Who wanted power—your mother?'

'Good God, no; she wanted peace. But Grandmother Searle was relentless, my mother weak; she took tranquilisers then started drinking, and the more she drank, the more I turned to Grandmother, so the more she drank. It was a vicious circle.'

'It's hardly your fault, is it?' Vanessa said, seeing that he felt guilty. She too had suffered that, blaming herself for her parents' attitude towards her even though she knew that their flares of temper had been unwarranted.

'I don't know; I'll never know—like I'll never know whether she meant to take her own life or whether it was an accident. She may have taken the extra tablets without realising she had already taken the prescribed amount; I just don't know.'

The anguish in his voice and the bright shimmer of unshed tears that filled his eyes made Vanessa leap to his side. She wrapped her arms around him, pulling him close to her, the scent of him filling her nostrils. There was nothing sexual in her action; it was just a very natural human response to his distress. He welcomed her attention, melting against her soft body, and she held him tightly, trying to ease the pain she knew he was feeling.

'It's the never knowing that hurts me, never having a chance to make amends, to ask forgiveness,' he explained.

'Forgiveness?' questioned Vanessa. She didn't understand; he'd started off by saying that he hated his parents and finished with wanting his mother's forgiveness.

'She tried to tell me, to explain, but I wouldn't listen; I only ever listened to Grandmother Searle,' he said bitterly, pushing himself away from Vanessa and sitting up to tell her more. But she hadn't wanted him to move. She'd been enjoying the quiet strength of his body resting on her, the closeness that was intimate but not threatening.

'My mother wouldn't give her shares up; she refused to go along with Grandmother's plans for the company. She didn't believe in using people like that Grandmother wanted to make huge numbers of staff redundant to increase the profits, and when my mother refused she used me, only I was too foolish to see it.'

'So how did you find out?' Vanessa asked.

'I was to marry Vicky Standford; I thought she loved

me though my mother kept saying I was falling into the same trap she had. But I didn't listen; all I saw was a weak fool who took comfort in drink and drugs.'

'You mean Vicky didn't love you?' Vanessa gasped. She couldn't comprehend that; the other woman had seemed so keen on him.

'Yes. All she wants is to be part of the Knight Corporation: she's now after Robert and he'll fall into the trap,' he said bitterly.

'How do you know all this? Surely you're just guessing?' she offered. It all sounded rather strange to her—a whole set of people ruled by this one despot who was prepared to destroy them all for control of a company.

'I know it sounds unbelievable but it's true. After my mother's death I cleared her papers; it was then I discovered the truth.' He stood up and marched over to the window, gazing out into the dark night as he struggled with his emotions. His body was tense, racked with an inner pain that had been turned into anger.

'What did you find?'

'Letters from my grandmother demanding that my mother sign the shares over to her—insulting, rude letters, including the final one my grandmother sent her in her moment of triumph. She warned my mother that now that she had successfully arranged my marriage to Vicky I would automatically become responsible for the shares and therefore she was now surplus to requirements. At first I couldn't believe it, but when I thought about it it all made sense. Vicky had been groomed for me; she knew my likes and dislikes, favourite authors, eating habits. . . It was all too pat, too simple, so I asked her, confronted her with the truth.'

'And?'

'At first she denied it but when I persisted she said that Grandmother had approached her with a deal that was hard to refuse; besides she pointed out, if it didn't work we could just get a quicky divorce.' He gave a hollow, scornful laugh as he swung round to meet Vanessa's understanding gaze.

'That's quite a story,' she breathed, knowing how hard it must have been for him to tell her all that. 'It seems Robert missed quite a bit out in the profile.'

'I guess so, but there's a lot even Robert doesn't know,' he informed her, stifling a yawn. 'I'm shattered,' he confessed.

'Emotionally drained?' Vanessa smiled as he slumped back into a chair.

'I suppose so—I've never told anybody about my family. Anyway, that's why I went away; I needed time alone to sort myself out, to decide what I wanted from life,' he explained, and yawned again, placing his hand over his mouth.

'You can stay the night,' she offered without thinking. Ryan's eyebrows rose at the invitation and a wicked smile sprang immediately to his lips. 'On the couch,' she added crisply, but was unable to stop herself responding to his smile, matching it with one of her own.

'That would be great,' he said, shrugging off his jacket, pulling at his tie and kicking off his shoes.

Watching him, Vanessa began to doubt the wisdom of her decision. He looked far too comfortable, too much at home, and his presence was strangely disturbing.

'Can I take a shower before I crash out?' he asked, bending down and removing his socks.

'Of course,' agreed Vanessa, watching his every move like a nervous kitten. 'It's through there,' she said, pointing down the hall. 'I'll get you some bedding,' she added, moving with alacrity. She wanted him settled quickly so she could hide away in her bedroom.

It took her just a few minutes to grab some bedding, and she was on her way to her room as Ryan opened the bathroom door. He paused as he saw her, shaking his damp hair from his face like a dog. He had tied a bathtowel around his hips but apart from that he was naked, his bare body glistening with droplets of water. Vanessa's eyes were automatically drawn to the bronze expanse of his chest, taking in the smoothness of his skin and the well-defined muscles that her fingers itched to touch.

She braced herself to ward him off as he moved towards her, fighting an inner battle between desire and fear. He gave a low, careless laugh as he saw her conflict but made no attempt to touch her, though she could feel the powerful tug of his attraction for her.

'I'd best go to bed,' he said, his voice husky, his tone sending tremors down her spine, but she feigned indifference.

'Good idea. Goodnight, Ryan.' She forced a smile to her lips. 'Sleep well.'

'And you,' he murmured, before he brushed his firm lips quickly over hers and then drew back, a seductive smile curling the corners of his mouth.

Vanessa quickly lowered her lids over her eyes so that he would not see the invitation in them, which she knew would be shining from the very depths of her being. She had seen a side of him tonight that had only increased her desire for him and yet she wondered if she would ever share the pain of her own childhood with anyone. She knew he was still curious, and with their engagement party looming she would have to come up with some suitable story.

She closed the bedroom door, thinking about her past, and as she fell asleep the haunting memories came back in a series of terrifying nightmares. . .

The darkness enveloped her as she was pushed deeper into the cupboard, and when her protests were ignored she kicked hard at the closing door, but her action was futile and hot, bitter tears of rage and fear poured down her cheeks.

'Stop that racket or you'll get a taste of me belt, then I'll know why you're crying,' the drunken voice shouted as he kicked hard at the closed door, his words silencing her. She stuffed her clenched fist into her mouth, her teeth sinking into her knuckles as she tried to stifle her sobs, and she rocked herself backwards and forwards and tried hard to think of something else.

Suddenly she felt his hands on her, pulling her, drawing her up away from the blackness that had become her refuge.

'No!' she cried, her head thrusting right and left in protest as she struggled for her freedom. 'No, no, no,' she protested as her body was dragged from the warmth.

'Vanessa! Vanessa!' The voice was sharp. 'Wake up. Wake up!' it demanded, and Vanessa gasped as her eyes slowly began to focus. Beads of nervous sweat trickled down her spine, dampening her nightshirt, and it clung to her body revealingly.

'I had a nightmare,' she explained.

'I guessed,' Ryan said grimly, watching her with an

intent that was disconcerting. 'A recurring one?' he probed gently, and Vanessa nodded mutely, closing her eyes against the grim images that still flew in front of her face. 'Want to talk about it?' he asked, but Vanessa knew she couldn't so she shook her head. Ryan rose to his feet, but Vanessa reached out and grabbed his arm; she felt his muscle ripple under her touch.

'Please don't go,' she pleaded. 'Stay with me.' Her eyes were wide with fear, her heart still thudding against her chest. It had been so long since she'd had that dream that she'd thought it had gone for ever, but now it had returned with a vengeance and it made her feel like the same trapped child she had been then—alone and unloved.

Ryan looked down at her and could see the pain and fear in her eyes.

'Move up, then,' he said, and climbed onto the bed beside her and lay down next to her. Vanessa closed her eyes, reassured by his presence. She'd thought she'd be too aware of him but the slow, steady rhythm of his deep breathing made her relax and within moments she had drifted back to sleep, where her nightmare waited to claim her again. She was aware of someone crying— could hear soft, gentle sobs. A warm, strong arm wrapped around her and her head fell as delicately as a snowdrop onto a hard chest and rested there till it grew wet with tears.

Vanessa pulled her head away, suddenly aware of what was happening—that it was she who was crying, that the tears were hers and that she was resting on Ryan. Her cheeks were flushed and she stared open-mouthed at Ryan, who had now propped himself up on his elbow and was looking at her with sternly questioning eyes.

'I think you'd better talk about it,' he told her in an oddly gentle tone that was nonetheless underlined with a ring of authority that told her it was more a command than a suggestion.

'It was Kevin,' she said flatly, then turned away as her body trembled at the mention of his name. She had never wanted to speak it again and now he had permeated her own home, spoiling it, tainting it with his dirty presence. She wondered if she would ever be free of him.

'Kevin?' he repeated, hating the fact that he didn't know who Kevin was—was he an uncle, brother, friend or lover?

'He came to live with my mother when I was about six. I didn't like him.' She shuddered at the crystal-clear memory of his unshaven, leering face and Ryan drew her back into his arms.

'You're shivering.' He pulled her closer to him so that her spine was pressed against his stomach. Vanessa made no objection; there was consolation in his action, a gentleness she had not expected. They both lay in silence—a silence that was thick with unspoken emotion, charged with all the pent-up feelings that were tearing at Vanessa's soul.

Finally she could bear it no longer.

'He hurt me,' she sobbed. 'He hurt me.'

Rage, red-hot rage, directed at a man he didn't even know, surged uncontrollably through Ryan's body, and it took all his powers of self-control to say calmly, 'How did he hurt you?'

Vanessa groaned as a fresh series of tremors swept

through her body and the bitter taste of shame scorched the back of her throat; instinctively she drew up her knees, curling herself into a ball. She felt Ryan's hand slowly slide down the length of her hair, the repetitious stroking action soothing her.

'He'd get drunk. Most of the time he was all right, then he'd get drunk and...' She faltered as a fresh series of painful sobs racked her body and the tears for all those years that she had stored away began to fall.

'He was violent,' offered Ryan, hating the thought of someone deliberately hurting someone else—especially a child, especially Vanessa. She nodded as the tears fell hot and burning from her swollen eyes and she shivered as she rubbed her hands up and down her bare arms. Ryan pulled the quilt back over the pair of them, waiting for her to say more.

'Come on, Vanessa; you've been very brave even to mention it. Let's talk it all out; tell me more,' he whispered, one arm still wrapped around her waist, holding her to him, whilst his other hand reassuringly stroked her hair, lulling her into his confidence.

'I was nearly sixteen, going to my first disco at school. I wanted to look special...' Her voice faded as the familiar fear stirred in the pit of her stomach. 'I'd never worn make-up or a proper dress and I wanted to look grown-up...' She sobbed again, the sick dread of that moment flashing into her mind. 'He said I looked pretty, very pretty, and then he...he...'

Her voice broke and she shuddered, the feeling of revulsion taking over. She could feel his hands on her, inquisitive, searching, pulling at her, shame and the pain as real as ever.

'Oh, my God.' Ryan bit back the explosion of expletives that rushed into his mind. This was no time for self-indulgence. 'My poor little Nessie,' he crooned. 'You poor baby.' He rested his head on hers, his breath warm on her face, and wiped away the damp tears as he rocked her to and fro, nursing her as if she were a baby in need of comfort.

'It wasn't my fault, it wasn't my fault,' she managed to say between sobs, and Ryan silently cursed the man who had done this to her and left her with so much guilt and pain.

'Of course not; no one thinks that,' he reassured her. 'It's all right now; you'll be all right.'

'I pushed him away, I didn't let him touch me, but I could tell I was no longer safe—I could see it in his eyes—so I ran away,' she confessed, sitting up in the bed and wrapping her arms around her bent knees. 'I always send them a Christmas card but I've never let them know where I am; I don't suppose they're interested anyway,' she concluded sadly, because there was still a part of her that needed them.

Ryan propped himself up on his elbow, looking at her. Her hair had fallen in disarray around her slim shoulders and her eyes were wide with fear and swollen with crying. Her nightshirt made her look like a child in an adult's shirt, she looked so small and soft and delicate; the thin veneer of sophistication had been shattered.

'Where did you go?' he asked, intrigued that despite her vulnerability she was so strong—a survivor against all the odds that life had stacked against her.

'I moved to another city, lived rough for a couple of months then managed to get in a hostel. From there I used my brains to help me escape. University was so easy for me—I was never homesick and always able to manage—just—on my grant,' she told him, and the evident pride in her voice made him smile.

'You've done well, very well, and telling me was a first step—' he began, but she cut in, the alarm in her voice tangible.

'What do you mean, first step?' There was a trace of anxiety in her tone, and her arms tightened around her knees for comfort.

'Counselling. There are lots of places you can go to for help.'

'I'm OK. I don't need help; I've coped.' She pushed her hand through her hair in a gesture of agitation and scrambled from the bed. 'I don't want to talk about it; it's all in the past,' she grated, regretting telling him as much as she had; she didn't want this type of pressure.

'It will never be in the past,' he told her as he joined her at her side. She was aware of every inch of him; he exuded a sexual aura without any effort. She held her body rigid—her only defence against the logic of his argument.

'You can't bury all that pain away, or the hurt and confusion and anger you must feel. It's all there, deep inside you,' he said, his face showing an inner wisdom.

'I'm all right; I really don't need this Freudian psychology,' she said, hating this intrusion; she was not ready for any sort of therapy.

He clasped her by the shoulders and spun her round; she recognised his anger and tried to pull away but his grip held firm.

'You're still trapped—trapped by the past—and you'll never escape, never fully escape, until you face up to it, confront all your worst fears. Get help.'

She averted her eyes from his unnerving icy glare, shook herself free and marched away, going to the kitchen to make a drink; the chance of sleep now was remote and she didn't feel in the least tired. She knew he had followed her; though his bare feet had made no sound she could sense his presence, even catch the scent of him, she was so aware of him.

'Tea?' she offered, her voice flat and emotionless as she tossed two bags into a pot.

'I'm trying to help you,' he said, touching her arm with an odd combination of strength and tenderness, but she drew away.

'I don't want or need your help,' she protested, glaring at him, her eyes molten pools of outrage at his suggestion as she struggled to hide her deeper pain behind a façade of indifference and anger.

'Ten minutes ago you were crying in my arms like a baby,' he reminded her firmly, ignoring the sudden pain that flickered in her eyes. 'You wanted and needed me then,' he told her forcefully.

'I had a nightmare; it's passed, gone, and is best forgotten,' she tossed at him, busying herself with tea-making to avoid his expression, which she knew would be disapproving.

'And how often does that nightmare come? How often are you alone making cups of tea in the early hours of the morning?' he persisted, and Vanessa held the sugar spoon over her cup as she paused to reflect on his words. He gauged her reaction and continued, 'Rid yourself of those nightmares, Vanessa, because if you don't you're never going to be free.'

She spun round, hating the truth of his words. 'Are you free, Ryan—free of all your bitterness towards your

family, free of all the guilt and pain you feel?' she flung
at him, enjoying a moment of triumph as a stunned
look quickly shadowed his face.

'Not entirely,' he admitted calmly. 'But I'm working
on it,' he added guardedly as he picked up a cup of tea
and took a sip. Vanessa watched him closely; there was
no anger in him though she knew she had treated him
badly.

'I'm sorry,' she blurted out. 'I appreciate your concern but I'm quite capable of looking after myself,' she
told him, tilting her chin upwards in an attempt to
appear in control and strong.

'Are you?' he asked, his tone bland, but amusement
danced in his eyes.

'Yes,' she replied emphatically, picking up her cup,
and went back into the living room, Ryan following,
hot on her heels.

'You're such a bad liar.' He laughed, slumping down
on the couch next to her, and absently picked up the
remote control and flicked on the television. An old
black and white horror film leapt onto the screen with
a blood-curdling cry. Vanessa jumped at the sudden
noise and he noted her reaction but said nothing.
Vanessa seethed inwardly.

'These films are always good for a laugh,' she said,
tucking her legs underneath her and settling down to
watch.

'You watch a lot of films at this time of night?' he
asked casually, drinking his tea and keeping his eyes
fixed firmly on the screen.

'If I wake up I tend to tune in,' she admitted before
she realised what she was saying, and when she flashed
him a look the smile of superiority was wide across his

face. She gave a sigh. She could deny it again but it would be futile so instead she feigned a complete and total interest in the film, although she was already feeling drowsy.

'Come on, sleepyhead, you'd best go to bed.' Ryan helped her to her feet and her head fell against his chest. She could hear his heart thudding against her ear; the sound was comforting.

'I can't imagine why I'm so sleepy; usually I'm a real night owl,' she said.

'It's probably the champagne you drank, especially with you not being used to it,' he told her. He felt warm, strong, yet his skin was so soft that she wanted to touch it, to feel it beneath her fingers. She stumbled wearily as he held her and looked up to apologise; their faces were so close that she could barely make out his features but she could feel the slumberous warmth in his eyes, feel the rapid beating of his heart.

'Come on,' he said, and Vanessa felt a momentary disappointment before she fell onto the bed and closed her eyes. He clasped her legs, swung them up onto the bed, and pulled the quilt over her.

'Stay with me?' she pleaded, wrapping a restraining arm around his neck and drawing him down towards her.

He shook his head. 'Somehow I don't think that would be a good idea.'

'Yes, it would,' Vanessa insisted. 'I might have another nightmare.'

'I'll be in the next room; just shout if you need me,' he told her calmly, but she sensed his strain and smiled at the power she had just learnt she possessed.

'Goodnight, Ryan,' she whispered, half-asleep and oblivious to the invitation she had just given.

'Goodnight, Vanessa,' he replied in a whisper, then he leant across and planted a soft kiss on her lips.

Ryan tried to settle on the couch but he was tormented with thoughts and images of Vanessa—not just of her terrible childhood but also the beautiful image he had just left sleeping, soft, warm and seductive, with a smile that could melt the stoniest of hearts. He frowned when he thought of how he was deceiving her but when he explained it all to her she would understand—wouldn't she?

CHAPTER NINE

VANESSA paused and leant back in her chair, forgetting about her work for the moment. So much had been happening in her life recently. It was two weeks since she and Ryan had discussed their backgrounds and since then there had been an indefinable change in their relationship. They were closer, working together as a team, and the attraction they felt for each other seemed to grow stronger every day. Vanessa's heart leapt at the thought.

She was also seeing a counsellor. The relief of being able to discuss her past was almost physical; she felt as if a heavy burden was being lifted from her shoulders. She felt different; she couldn't really describe how, but knew she was more relaxed, happier. She'd hated talking to a stranger at first but her counsellor was so kind that a rapport had soon been built up and now Vanessa felt she could trust her completely.

She had been surprised at just how much she had been bottling up; incidents she had thought she had completely forgotten about had come bubbling back to the surface in a cocktail of pain and anger. She had been going to therapy three times a week, and her counsellor was of the opinion that now, after her fifth visit, she was well on the road to recovery.

But Vanessa knew that herself. Her own attitude had changed; most of her anger towards the adults she'd grown up with was slowly being replaced with emotions of pity. She knew that to a great extent she had Ryan to thank for that but she had not even mentioned the fact that she was going to therapy; she was still a little nervous about admitting it.

'Hi. Penny for them?' Ryan smiled as he popped his head around the door.

'Hi, yourself,' Vanessa responded, quickly pushing all her thoughts to the back of her mind.

'Are you all set for tonight?' He grinned as he came into her office and began to help himself to a coffee. Vanessa shook her head as he offered her a cup.

'I suppose so, but imagine the hassle afterwards, the presents we will have to send back. It'll be a nightmare.' She frowned at the thought. It was all so deceitful; she hated tricking everyone.

'I know you disapprove of the whole thing, so perhaps we'll just have to stay engaged, even marry.' He smiled his brightest smile; it was full of warm, sensual invitation and amusement danced in the depths of his silvery gaze.

'I don't think so,' Vanessa retorted sharply, hating the fact that her stomach had flipped at the thought.

'Why not? I think we'd make a good team,' he said, leaning his hip on her desk as he spoke, his tone more serious now.

'You romantic fool,' she teased. 'You certainly know how to sweep a girl off her feet. "We'd make a good team",' she repeated, wrinkling her nose in distaste, unaware of how attractive it made her look. Ryan reacted immediately, falling to his knees at her side and clasping her hand tightly, raising it to his lips and kissing it tenderly.

'My darling,' he crooned, his voice low and husky

and thick with a pseudo French accent. 'I love you; you know that. Be mine or my life will be meaningless,' he said with a sob.

Vanessa laughed at his actions despite the sharp pain that his humour inflicted on her. She knew she was slowly falling in love with him. Against all the odds she had grown to love him over the past few weeks.

'Your life *is* meaningless,' she reminded him as he climbed back to his feet.

'Shall I take that as a no, then?' he asked, and for a moment he looked genuinely disappointed.

'Take it as a maybe.' She smiled though her heart was already beginning to crack with the strain of remaining just friends.

'You sound as romantic as me,' he complained, picking up his coffee, his eyes still fixed on her.

'You're right—I'm not,' she confessed, hating the way he was looking at her; his silvery eyes seemed to pierce her innermost thoughts and feelings. There was a hint of sadness in her tone that he picked up on and he allowed a secret smile to cross his face. 'What are you smiling at?' she asked with a frown, but he shook his head in reply. Vanessa guessed he was up to something.

'I'm stuck,' she admitted, pushing a pile of papers filled with figures over to him. She preferred to keep their conversations confined to work though it was becoming increasingly difficult. Ryan constantly changed the subject, steering it on to a more personal level.

'The only figure I can concentrate on when I'm with you is yours.'

'Will you be serious for once? We're getting nowhere

fast here,' she scolded, hiding her pleasure behind a disapproving look.

'I am serious; I think you've got a marvellous figure.' He allowed his hand to glide gently down her back and rest on her hip. Vanessa's stomach clenched at his touch, a flicker of sudden sexual excitement spiralling through her body, making her feel weak.

'This is sexual harassment,' she reminded him, but she did not move his hand; she was enjoying the feel of it too much.

'Rubbish! We are attending our engagement party tonight,' he replied, his voice falling to a deep, dark rumble, and his eyes looked deep into hers, weakening any arguments she still had.

'Can you try and concentrate on this?' she asked. Her own emotions were running high and she knew the only cure was work. 'I've found something out, something very important,' she told him.

He was listening now. His hand dropped from her side and she felt the chill to her skin as he moved away slightly, his eyes fixed firmly on the papers.

'What is it?' he asked, his eyes scanning the details, a trace of alarm in his voice.

'You told me your aunt Karen sold her shares back to the company but I've discovered she kept quite a large number as an investment,' Vanessa began to explain, and instantly a deep frown creased his forehead and he thrust his hand through his hair, raking it back from his stern face.

'So? What difference does it make?'

'Quite a big difference if she sells to our mystery buyer, because then he would have control of the company,' she finished triumphantly.

Ryan stared at her, his eyes icing over, as hard and clear as diamond chips.

'Are you sure? You have checked every single share she has?' he asked, his voice as flat and emotionless as the expression on his face.

'That's what I'm asking you to do—double-check— but I really do think we're on to something here,' she said, enthusiasm bubbling over.

'She wouldn't sell,' he said dismissively, and Vanessa's heart sank. 'I'll check the figures and let you know.'

'Thanks. Meanwhile I'll try and get in touch with Karen,' she said, settling back down in her chair to commence work.

'No!' he cried. 'Let's check the figures first. Besides, if anyone approached Karen surely she'd tell Robert? He is her son, remember,' he told her as he sauntered to the door.

'I guess so,' agreed Vanessa, but a niggling doubt festered at the back of her mind. She had been so sure. A gut instinct was still telling her she was right but she had to agree with Ryan—it seemed highly unlikely that a mother would deliberately undermine her son's business interests.

She sighed as she looked back down at all her papers. There must be something else—something she had not noticed. There must be a clue somewhere, she thought as she began to sift through all the information she had collated.

Vanessa tried to stifle the butterflies that whirled in her stomach; she couldn't understand why she felt so nervous. She glanced again at the clock and tutted impatiently—trust Ryan to be late tonight of all nights.

They had been seeing each other every evening for the past few weeks to help along the idea that they were totally in love, and he had never once been late, but of course tonight he was.

She frowned as she heard the unusual sound of horse's hooves outside. She would have looked out of the window to see what was going on but at that moment her intercom buzzed. She grabbed her coat, flicked off the lights and made her way to the door.

'At last!' she grumbled as she opened the door to an immaculately dressed Ryan, her heart stopping briefly at the sight of him. Her reactions to him seemed to be growing stronger every day. He looked so handsome, his bronzed skin contrasting golden against his white shirt. His hair shone under her hall light and her fingers longed to touch it, to feel it fall through her fingers.

'What a delightful welcome.' He smiled, unperturbed by her hostility, as with a flourish he drew a huge bouquet of white flowers from behind his back.

'White frangipani!' she gasped. 'Where on earth did you get these?' she asked, stunned by the beautiful bouquet.

'I had them flown in from our island. How's that for romantic?' he teased, delighted by her reaction.

Vanessa felt the hot stab of pinpricks burn the back of her eyes and she flung herself into his arms. These were the flowers Patimo had given her as a garland the first time she and Ryan had gone to dinner together.

'Mind the flowers,' he said, but she silenced his objections with a tender kiss.

'Come on, there's more,' he said as she drew back, and he took her hand.

'What about the flowers?' she asked.

'They will keep,' he told her, tightening his grip, sending a series of delightful tremors up her arm. Vanessa put the bouquet down on the hall table and slammed the door behind her as she was dragged outside.

'Ryan!' she cried as she stared in total surprise at the horse-drawn carriage that awaited them. The coachman leapt from his seat and opened the carriage door, pulled down the step and extended his hand out to Vanessa. She smiled her thanks as she climbed aboard and Ryan sat next to her, his thigh brushing against her leg.

'New outfit?' he asked, his eyes skimming over her, warming her body with his heated gaze.

'I thought it was appropriate to buy something new for one's engagement,' she teased, delighted by the effort he had gone to to make the evening special.

'It's not your usual style,' he said with a wicked grin, his eyes trailing with undisguised interest up the length of leg Vanessa was showing.

'I felt like a change,' she admitted, knowing that it was because of her counselling sessions that she had now started feeling more confident—that and all the attention Ryan had been giving her. Her sexual confidence had been growing too and she knew she looked very sexy with this new look she had chosen. She was wearing a tight-fitting mini-dress in black Lycra, cut away deeply at the back. Her hair had been scooped up high on her head then allowed to fall in a cascade of curls. The overall effect was stunning.

'I like it; everyone will be amazed at the beauty of my fiancée—and the fact that she has brains as well!' His hand fell suggestively on her thigh but she made no attempt to move it. She was incensed by his sexist remark.

'They are not mutually exclusive,' she complained. 'A woman can have both.'

'And it's a very dangerous combination,' he whispered, his voice thick and hoarse with frustrated intimacy. His long fingers began to trail a path further up her leg, causing a series of tiny tremors to shiver through her body. Vanessa's mouth went dry as her body began to dissolve into a sea of pleasure that she had never experienced before.

She lifted her face to his in silent invitation; she wanted to feel his mouth on hers, hot and demanding. She readied herself for his onslaught, the hunger and passion that were always present in their kisses. But tonight his mouth was gentle, soft and pliant. His lips whispered over hers in a heady promise that there was more to come and her body melted against his.

A gasp of surprise escaped from the back of her dry throat as he caught her face in his hands. His action only increased her desire; she felt wanted, loved, and she was responding in a way she had never imagined possible. She raised her arms to his neck, clasping him tightly and drawing him down towards her. Their kiss intensified, deepened as their passion rose in unison.

They were breathless when they drew apart, their eyes still locked together, shining with all the unspent passion that was still charging through their bodies.

'I want to make love to you.'

A tremor shuddered throughout her body at his words. She wasn't sure. She knew she loved him but it was a big step; besides, did he really care for her or was she merely convenient? She smiled as an idea struck her. If she could make him jealous, see the way he reacted when she was with other men, maybe then she could be sure of his feelings towards her.

'You'll be all right; you're the guest of honour,' Ryan told her when Vanessa faltered as she caught her first glimpse of the Searles' family home.

'I had no idea...' she began as she gazed at the huge solid stone house. It was Georgian; two huge white pillars made an impressive focal point and a pair of oak doors were fully open, revealing a beautifully tiled hall. A huge crystal chandelier glittered from an ornate ceiling. Music drifted from the open doors and the hum of conversation hung in the air.

'I can't,' she proclaimed, pulling back and ducking her head back into the carriage as waves of fear swept over her.

'You have to; besides, I want to show you off.' He grinned, pulling her from the carriage, and she fell heavily against him. He was badly winded but still managed to catch her, fully enjoying the soft feel of her delicate body as he held her in his arms.

She leaned into him, her longing for him outstripping any fears. She felt him stiffen slightly as she pressed her body against his, enjoying the power she had over him. He reluctantly lowered her to the ground and she remained where she was, looking up into his face.

There was something in his expression that was strangely compelling; there seemed to be some kind of hidden message behind his mask of control. She shivered in anticipation but for now they had to act the role of devoted couple, though as Ryan clasped her hand Vanessa knew that for her part it was no longer an act.

The interior of the house was equally grand as the

outside, with an understated elegance that could only be acquired with a vast amount of wealth. It certainly put Vanessa's family background in the shade. She smoothed down her dress as her coat was removed and then was introduced to so many people that afterwards she could not remember a single name.

'Here. You look as if you could do with a drink.'

Vanessa turned, surprised that the gesture of friendship was being made by Vicky. She looked at the dubiously coloured liquid.

'What is it?' she asked.

'Fruit punch for the drivers,' she told her, sipping at a glass of champagne. 'You don't drink, do you?' She smiled without warmth.

'Not really. Ryan has been trying to introduce me to some wines but I'm still a novice,' she confessed, taking a taste of her drink and screwing up her nose. 'It tastes odd.'

'Passion fruit.'

'Oh, I see,' she nodded.

'Your parents didn't make it, then?' Vicky asked, a dangerous gleam flickering in her eyes.

'No, they are out of the country,' Ryan intervened, putting a protective arm across Vanessa's shoulders.

'Really? Then you haven't met Vanessa's family yet? It will be quite a surprise, then, when you do.' She grinned maliciously and Vanessa found it hard to suppress a shudder at her words.

'Ignore her. It's sour grapes because I am marrying you instead of her,' Ryan said, and Vanessa stared at him open-mouthed, her eyes wide with surprise.

'But Ryan—' she began, but he had already been

swallowed up by a rowdy group of friends who hadn't seen him in ages.

'Care to dance?' offered a friendly young man who Vanessa vaguely recognised as someone who worked in the accounts department. She smiled and threw back her drink, grimacing as the aftertaste burned her throat. She guessed then that it must have contained alcohol and she wondered why Vicky should have been so thoughtless. Still, it had given her the courage to dance. The music was fast and lively and Vanessa joined in with gusto, enjoying the thudding beat as it drummed through her ears, making her feel quite excited.

When the music changed to a slower tempo Vanessa was glad of the rest; her breathing was rapid and her heart thudding with the exertion. Mark, the man from Accounts, placed his arms around her waist, swaying with her to the music, and Vanessa closed her eyes as she rested, unaware that she was being watched.

Ryan's eyes narrowed on the couple, watching their movements with interest, and as Mark's hand began to descend down Vanessa's back he marched across the dance-floor and gripped Vanessa by the wrist in a painful grip. She gave a cry of pain as he wrenched her away from Mark's side, casting him a freezing look as he did so. Vanessa smiled in triumph. It was just the sort of reaction she'd wanted.

'You shouldn't be dancing like that,' Ryan whispered fiercely, his eyes dark with frustration and anger.

'Why not?' Vanessa smiled, her chin tilted upwards in challenge. 'Jealous?' she asked, her eyes wide with innocence.

'Don't be ridiculous; of course not,' he protested, still glaring at her. 'But for the sake of appearances you should hardly be wrapped round another man,' he growled.

'I was hardly wrapped around him; we were merely dancing,' she retorted, more angry with herself for so foolishly thinking that he cared for her than she was with him.

'Come off it, I saw you,' he snapped, his eyes searing her with their intensity.

'Saw what?' she declared in indignation. 'We were just dancing,' she repeated through clenched teeth.

'Now, now, children,' purred a smug voice at the side of them.

'Go away, Vicky,' snapped Ryan. 'This happens to be a private conversation.'

'I'm sure Vanessa's heard quite enough of your caveman views; besides, I've a little surprise for her,' she said, taking Vanessa by the hand, and she proceeded to lead her through the hall to the library.

'In there, Vanessa.'

Vanessa turned with a puzzled look on her face but Vicky had already left her, giving her a tiny wave as she disappeared back into the main hall. Vanessa paused for a moment then pushed open the door and walked in, closing the door behind her.

It was dim inside. There was a table lamp in the corner and it threw a shadowy light over the chair beside the fireplace. Vanessa gasped, her heart sinking; she felt as if she had been kicked in the stomach and instinctively her hands flew there as she stared at her nightmare in the chair.

'Done well for yourself, haven't you?' He grinned, displaying a row of brown, tobacco-stained teeth as his eyes trailed over her, making her flesh crawl.

'What do you want?' she demanded, forcing herself to relax as she began to feel like a little girl again, frightened and alone.

'Now that's a lovely greeting for your father after all this time,' he said, taking another large mouthful of his drink then wiping the back of his hand across his mouth.

Vanessa watched in horror; it was all so sickly familiar. He looked older but still as strong, despite the fact that his face was riddled with the red spider's web of a chronic drinker, and his eyes looked as glassy and sharp as ever.

'Stepfather,' she corrected him. 'That's if you ever bothered to marry,' she concluded grimly as she looked round for her mother, expecting to see her slumped in another chair somewhere.

'Married or not, I was the only father you ever had,' he said with a cruel smile, tossing back his drink and getting up to help himself to another. His gait was awkward; the years of alcohol abuse had taken their toll and the effects on his body were evident. He looked shorter, his shoulders rounded and bent.

'Where is she?' Vanessa asked. She had to know, and a trickle of fear ran down her spine as the thought occurred to her that her mother might have died.

'We're not together any more. She got religious,' he spluttered, his tone halfway between laughter and disgust. 'She went on the wagon. . .' His contempt for Vanessa's mother's new life was evident but Vanessa wasn't interested in listening to his attack.

'Where is she?' she demanded.

'I dunno; she went to live with her sister in a boarding 'ouse on the coast somewhere,' he said, making a careful inventory of the valuables around him. 'You done really well, girlie,' he slurred.

'What's the name of the place?' persisted Vanessa.

'I dunno, but she does.'

'Who?'

'That Standford woman. She traced me and yer mum but yer mum wouldn't come; gave her some tale about feeling guilty—though what she has to feel guilty about I dunno. You did all right.'

'No thanks to you,' threw back Vanessa, all the hatred she felt for him welling up inside her.

'Don't take that attitude wiv me, lady,' he suddenly snarled, spinning round, his eyes blazing with a flare of anger that she recognised instantly.

Her stomach plummeted. She stepped back, panic pushing her heart into a more rapid, dangerous beat, and her mouth went dry, her throat tight and constricting as she struggled to breathe.

'You always did have a smart mouth,' he drawled, enjoying the power he had over her as he saw her step back, her eyes wide with fear.

The colour drained from her face; she felt sick with horror as he touched the buckle on his belt, fingering it as he stepped closer, tormenting her by his actions. Vanessa backed away, the beat of her heart thundering in her ears.

'That's enough.' Ryan's voice rapped out through his clenched teeth as he stepped from the shadows. Vanessa had been unaware that he had entered the room; all her senses had been trained on her stepfather.

'Who are you?' her stepfather demanded, hating the intrusion that had spoiled his fun.

'I think, since this is my home, that should be my question,' Ryan said, his voice chilling.

'I'm 'er father,' he said, a nervous tremor in his voice now that he had had time to assess the strength of his opponent and realised he was by far the weaker. He licked his lips to taste the whisky that would give him the confidence he needed.

'Out.' Ryan jerked his head towards the door as he pushed his hands deep into his trouser pockets in an attempt to control his desire to hit out at this animal.

'Look 'ere, you can't speak to me like that. I've come to see me daughter.'

But Ryan wasn't listening. He had heard enough already.

'Out—now,' he warned, his voice dangerously low and menacing. 'I shan't bother phoning the police,' he added, the threat clear, and the other man shifted uncomfortably.

'Here, Vanessa, you shouldn't let 'im speak to me like that,' he said, turning his attention back to Vanessa, who had been standing in silent shock, but his appeal fell on deaf ears.

'Just go,' she said, her voice weary. She felt sick. 'I never want to see you again,' she told him, her voice growing stronger now that Ryan was present.

'I was promised money—a lot of money,' he said greedily, his eyes flashing with a flare of annoyance. 'She said she'd give me money if I came here.'

'Victoria Standford?' asked Vanessa.

'Yeah, that's her. I want me money.' he said, his voice rough now that he saw the possibility of his being paid fading.

'Don't worry, she's leaving here now as well. You've

both outstayed your welcome,' Ryan said, stepping closer, his body radiating all his pent-up anger.

'I'm going,' Vanessa's stepfather snarled. 'You always were trouble, you,' he tossed at her. 'We were glad when you runned off,' he spat, and despite everything those words still managed to hurt her. She suppressed her anguish till he had left the room then sank, bewildered and stunned, into a chair and allowed her tears to fall.

It was some time before Ryan returned. She glanced up as he entered, and saw that he was looking a little dishevelled. He ran his fingers through his hair to tidy it and Vanessa guessed that her stepfather had taken a swing at him.

'Has he gone?' she asked, a spiral of renewed fear twisting inside her as she thought of him still being around.

'I don't think you'll see him again,' Ryan told her grimly, rubbing his hand over his scraped knuckles, and Vanessa gave him a faint smile of gratitude.

'I'm sorry,' she said suddenly as she choked on fresh tears. 'I'm so sorry.' The tears splashed down her face and he sank down on his haunches in front of her, clasping her hands.

'What have you got to be sorry about? It's hardly your fault,' he reassured her, but his kind gentleness only brought fresh tears and she shook her head. He produced a white linen handkerchief from his jacket and wiped her face. 'Here,' he said, giving it to her. 'I'll get you a drink.'

'Thanks,' she mumbled, and a few moments later accepted the brandy from him. The rich, heavy aroma made her pause as she raised the glass to her lips.

'Go on,' he encouraged.

Vanessa gave him a weak smile before taking a mouthful; it burned her throat before sending its warmth throughout her body, making her feel a little better.

'I want to go home.' She knew she sounded like a child at her first party but she couldn't bear the thought of facing anyone. The gossip would be awful and the careful image she had built up over the years had now been shattered.

'Good idea,' he agreed, getting to his feet. 'I'll bring the car round.'

'No, you'd best stay,' she said in sudden panic. 'What will people think?'

'Vanessa, do you honestly think I care about other people's opinions?' he asked with a roguish smile. 'Besides, you're my fiancée; if you have a headache it's only right and proper that I should see you home,' he told her firmly.

He returned moments later with her coat. 'I've made our apologies so we can make a quick getaway,' he explained. 'Luckily, I don't think anyone's that interested,' he added drily.

Vanessa smiled her thanks. Outside the car was waiting but she paused at the door, her eyes scanning the grounds.

'It's OK. He's gone—and, believe me, he won't be back.' He wrapped a comforting arm around her shoulder and escorted her to the car. She felt safe cocooned in the plush interior with Ryan—safe and secure.

She was still grateful, however, when he came up to her flat. She still felt a little nervous and unsure about being alone; it had been a terrible shock seeing her stepfather again.

'Are you OK?' he asked as he drew the curtains and flicked on the table lamp, its peach shade casting a warm glow on Vanessa's pale face.

'I think so. It was just that it all came back, all the black memories, and even though I'm an adult now part of me is still a child. Crazy, isn't it?' she said, pulling off her coat and kicking off her shoes before sinking onto the couch and tucking her long, slender legs underneath her.

'Part of us never grows up—and that man was frightening, believe me,' Ryan told her.

'What must people have thought. . .?' Vanessa began, distressed.

'Nothing. I told anyone who saw him that he was a disgruntled ex-employee and Vicky Standford won't dare to contradict me.' His mouth twisted in disgust at the mention of her name.

'Why did she do that?' Vanessa shook her head, unable to comprehend such bitterness towards her.

'Jealousy,' he explained as he sat down next to her, and he pulled off his shoes and tie and tossed them onto the floor.

'Jealous of me?' It was ridiculous.

'You have something she wants.'

'Me?'

'Yes,' he laughed, lifting her chin with his fingers to look at her full in the face. 'You have me,' he told her seriously, and Vanessa was speechless. She just stared at him, drowning in the depths of his warm, slumberous eyes.

'You believe me, don't you?' he asked, and when

Vanessa nodded mutely he smiled. 'Will you mention to your counsellor about him turning up?' he said as he began to peel off his socks.

Vanessa's heart stopped for a moment. That was all confidential; how did he know?

'I suppose so, but how do you know about that?' she asked, intrigued.

'When you were unable to see me till after nine two nights in a row I was suspicious.' He grinned, sitting back. 'So I followed you,' he admitted a little sheepishly.

'You followed me?' she repeated in disbelief. 'Why?'

'I wanted to see what or who was more important than me,' he confessed.

'Are you joking?'

'No. OK, I admit it; I was jealous,' he said, as if ashamed of the admission, but Vanessa's heart soared.

'I see,' she said, with a composure that took her by surprise. 'You were right—I did need to talk to some one. But I think I'm OK now. In fact seeing him tonight helped put certain things into perspective.'

'Good.'

'I might even go and see my mother,' she said, the idea suddenly coming to her.

'Clearview Boarding House,' Ryan said. 'I took the address from Vicky just in case she had any more surprises lined up. Here,' he said, offering her a crumpled bit of paper. Vanessa took it and stared at the address.

'How odd,' she said, half to herself. 'I don't even feel angry any more, just curious.' Her voice was soft and she sounded slightly puzzled.

'Will you go to see her?' he asked.

'Perhaps. But for now I just want to go to sleep. You'll stay?' she asked him, placing her hand over his arm. She still wanted to feel him close, needed the security his presence gave her.

'I wouldn't dream of leaving you,' he assured her with a sincere smile.

'Thanks.' And she leant over to plant a kiss on his cheek. He moved so that it landed on his lips and their kiss deepened to a dangerous level of intimacy. Vanessa drew back, alarmed by her reaction, her eyes filled with doubt and desire. She stared at Ryan for one very long minute. She was pleased that throughout the past few weeks he had made no attempt to pressurise her but now she felt different—ready to commit herself. She swallowed nervously and licked her dry lips.

'Let's go to bed.' They were the hardest words she had ever spoken and she thought she must have misread the signals when Ryan just stared at her.

'Me on the couch?' he asked dubiously, a puzzled frown creasing his forehead.

CHAPTER TEN

THERE was a moment when neither of them was quite sure what to do. They just sat there facing each other. Vanessa was fully aware of the gigantic step she was about to take but it seemed so right now—a natural part of their relationship.

'Vanessa. . .' he whispered in her ear, his breath soft and warm, and Vanessa closed her eyes to savour the sensation. 'Are you sure about this?' He drew back for a moment and studied her face with intent as he held her at arm's length.

'Yes, of course,' she answered, and for once in her life she was totally at peace with herself. There were no devils from her past driving her, forcing her to react in a certain way. She was herself—an adult, and fully prepared to make this commitment.

She stood up and raised her arms high above her head. 'You'll have to help—this dress fits like a second skin.' She laughed, and Ryan was only too eager to oblige.

The dress was peeled from her body and tossed carelessly to the floor and Vanessa stood before him in her finest lingerie, the smooth, shiny satin trimmed with the softest of French lace. She felt a momentary awkwardness before she felt Ryan's hand smooth over her shoulders and he murmured her name.

He drew her to him. His clothes now seemed like a harsh barrier and Vanessa's fingers began to undo his shirt. She revelled in the wonderful sensation of Ryan's skin and the ripple of his muscles as she trailed her fingers over his body, slowly moving her hand to his waist. She enjoyed the surge of power she felt when his stomach muscles tightened and she heard his sharp intake of breath.

The shirt was soon discarded and Vanessa helped him remove his trousers, pulling them down over his thighs, her hands running down the length of his legs. She wanted to feel every inch of his body. He slipped his hands underneath her arms and lifted her back up to him and they fell together onto the bed. She clasped his head in her hands, her fingers running through his hair, and she shuddered as she felt him draw closer to her, his body hard against her yielding softness.

She longed to feel his hands on her, strong, forceful, demanding, yet his touch was as gentle as a butterfly's wing, tentative and soft. His hands stroked over her body, making her stomach churn with anticipation and her blood race through her veins. His lips were soft and soothing and yet they held an underlying strength, a heady promise that still had to be fulfilled.

He removed the last pieces of her flimsy underwear with an expert's skill, and it was as if along with each article of clothing he stripped away all the pain of her past too. She knew her loneliness was gone for ever as she lay back, unable to speak the words of love that rose like a heavenly chorus from the depths of her being.

'You do trust me?' he asked her as he gazed down at her body, which was trembling beneath him.

'Of course I do.' Her face was soft with desire, her

hair a cloud of colour around her face. She could never doubt him. She loved him.

'Good; I need that,' he said, and covered her mouth with his lips, raising her from the bed as his desire deepened.

His strong arms wrapped around her, pulling her up against his raw strength, and she moaned as his head descended in a slow journey from her lips to her throat and, finally, to her breasts.

Her heart was racing, her body drowning in a sea of new sensations. He took hold of her breast, his thumb trailing over her erect, rosy nipple, and Vanessa's whole body shuddered with desire, her back arching. His mouth captured her breast, nipping and tugging then soothing with a firm kiss, till Vanessa felt as if she was suspended between a bridge of pain and pleasure, a heady mixture that left her breathless.

His hands trailed over her body, mapping every inch, and as his hand glided over her flat stomach the stab of anxiety that had stiffened her seemed to vanish as quickly as it had happened, hot, hungry desire replacing any doubts. She arched her back, pushing herself towards him, longing to feel him, but Ryan was in no hurry. He drew away, looking at her body with a heated gaze; it was pale in the moonlight, and so soft in contrast to his.

Vanessa smiled at him. At last she felt wanted, cherished, desired, and, above all, loved. She reached out to stroke the curve of his hip, the undulation of his back. He groaned at her touch and fell across her as she planted a series of kisses over his chest, her fingers now trailing down his back, clawing and demanding satisfaction.

She moaned as she felt his whole body descend over hers; she was trapped against her lover—her first and only lover—and the feeling was heavenly. Her body quivered in nervous anticipation but she felt ready for him, and offered herself willingly as he clasped her hips, drawing them up to meet him. There was no slowness now, no soothing gentleness; all his pent-up passion was spilling out.

Vanessa gave a cry as he entered her; she felt a hot, searing sensation, a dizzy combination of sharp, tingling pain and an unknown and as yet unfulfilled pleasure. His hips jerked back in surprise and he stopped as he stared wide-eyed at her.

'Vanessa?' he said, his voice sterner than she had expected at that moment, and her eyes shot open. She wondered what was wrong. 'I'm so sorry. I didn't realise, didn't think,' he confessed as he tried to draw back from her. Vanessa moved up against him, the pain having eased from her body, leaving her with a burning heat and a much deeper ache.

'I want to,' she invited softly, arching upwards to kiss him, and any chance of stopping was lost for ever. They moved in glorious unison, their hips grinding together, pounding against each other, and their cries filled the room before they finally sank from the heights they had touched back down onto the bed, still clasped together, locked in each other's embrace, their breathing ragged, blood pumping through their bodies.

'You should have told me,' Ryan said as he rolled away from her and drew her into his arms so that her head rested on his heaving chest, the drum of his heart like music in her ears.

'Why?' she asked simply, her body still burning with his touch, aching in all her most intimate places.

'I should have been gentler, more careful,' he confessed a little sadly, but Vanessa raised her head and kissed his mouth.

'It was perfect,' she said in a husky murmur, then sank back down and fell into a deep, much needed sleep. Ryan stroked his hand over her hair as he watched the gentle rise and fall of her body. He pulled the sheet up to cover her nakedness; it was too tempting to leave exposed, he thought with a wry smile.

It was an indescribable feeling for Vanessa, waking up to find herself locked within Ryan's arms; she felt that she belonged at last, that she was part of someone's life. She lay there savouring the moment, breathing in steady unison with him. Sunlight spilled across the unkempt bed—a reminder of last night's passion—and Vanessa moved tentatively, but her body felt totally refreshed and she smiled when she thought of his tender concern.

'You're awake, then?' he said, his arm tightening fractionally when she tried to move.

'Mmm,' she answered, lifting her face to look at him, her lips awaiting his kiss. She was not disappointed; the kiss was soft, warm and tender, and Vanessa pushed herself over his body. He gasped as her unexpected weight fell on him but the smile that lit up his face was the only invitation she needed.

'Shall we?' she asked, with an abandon she had never dreamt possible.

He threw a quick glance at the clock. 'Isn't it time for

work?' he said, pulling her down on top of him as he spoke.

'So I'll be late for once.' She grinned, and in that moment she knew she had changed for ever; her uptight, prissy image, her need to conform, to be always seen to do the right thing, had gone. The realisation was totally liberating and she laughed out loud, she felt so alive, so free. Ryan caught hold of her shaking body, joining in her laughter as it was so infectious.

The morning's lovemaking was taken at a lot slower pace than the night before's, each movement orchestrated so that both of them derived maximum pleasure from it. Finally they lay, fully satisfied, in each other's arms, drained of all emotion.

The tranquil moment was shattered by the incessant ringing of the phone. Vanessa reluctantly dragged herself from Ryan's arms and padded out of the room. She knew he was watching her and she smiled; she liked the fact that he enjoyed seeing her naked. She lifted the receiver, surprised when she heard Robert's voice, sharp and cutting. She listened in horror to his accusation; it hit at the very heart of her professionalism and was totally unwarranted.

As realisation slowly began to dawn, Vanessa felt her body ice over; her stomach dipped and she shut her eyes tightly against the tears that were fighting to spill down her face. She could barely put together a coherent sentence to answer Robert but she told him that she'd be in the office as soon as possible.

She put the receiver back down in its cradle with a shaking hand and shut her eyes. She felt sick. Ryan had used her. She had been a fool, had fallen so easily into his trap. How he must have laughed at her naïvety. It had been an act all along and she had been completely taken in by him.

She braced herself to face him, and suddenly her nakedness seemed abhorrent and out of place. She went straight to the bathroom and put on her towelling robe, then marched quickly into the bedroom. She wanted him out of her flat and out of her life—now.

Ryan had propped himself up against the pillows and he gave her a slow, languorous smile when she walked in, but she was immune now to his fatal charm.

'Get out!' she spat at him, her hatred for him blazing in her eyes. Her body was as tight as a coiled wire as she stared at him.

'What?' He was disorientated for a moment, unable to comprehend the pain and anger that were so blatant in her expression.

'I said, get out, and I mean it,' she repeated, a cold threat now present in her tone.

'Vanessa.' He scrambled from the bed to her side, but the freezing look she gave him prevented him from touching her. 'What is it?' he asked, but met a stone wall. 'For God's sake what is it?' He grabbed her arm but she shrugged herself free; his touch made her feel sick. It brought back the memory of how willingly she had given herself to him whilst he had betrayed her.

'Don't touch me!' she cried. 'Don't you dare lay a finger on me.' The anguish in her tone was coupled with anger and he drew back, troubled, as she turned from him.

'What is it? Who was that on the phone?' he demanded, his own anger stirring now.

'Robert,' she flung at him as she spun round, her eyes shimmering with unshed tears.

Ryan took a step back at the mention of his name. 'Robert. What did he say?'

'He accused me of being party to your scheme of deliberately misleading him, of withholding vital information,' she said curtly, spinning away from him to leave the room, but his hand shot out to prevent her, his own anger matching hers now. 'Get off me!' stormed Vanessa. Her stomach had flipped at his touch, she was still so vitally aware of him.

'You used me,' she spat at him through clenched teeth. 'I hate you!' And she wrenched herself free and slammed off into the bathroom, bolting the door behind her. Ryan followed, shouting her name.

'Vanessa! Vanessa!' He struck the door with his fist and it rattled its protest. 'Damn you, Vanessa, listen to me,' he shouted. 'You've got it wrong. Listen to me!' he demanded, but the only reply he received was the sound of the shower being turned on.

Vanessa heard him mumble a curse, and the slam of the front door as he left, but she stayed in the shower, trying to wash away all the shame and anger she felt. She wanted to cry, needed to cry, but she was too angry, too shocked. It was all a hideous nightmare; she couldn't believe it. She had to get to work to try and convince Robert that she had not been involved in Ryan's dealings.

Once she had showered she picked out her most sombre suit; it was a day for mourning, she thought grimly. She had lost her innocence in more than one way, she mused as she dressed with care, scooping her hair up into a severe style that did not in the least detract from her beauty. She arrived at work some twenty minutes later and went straight to her office; she stopped in her tracks as she opened her door.

'I want to talk to you,' Ryan began the moment she entered, raising himself from her chair.

'There's nothing to say,' Vanessa said, putting down her briefcase and shrugging off her coat. She kept her voice steady, her face expressionless; she was skilled at hiding her emotions—especially feelings of pain.

'You said you trusted me.' There was a plaintive ring to his tone that Vanessa heard but ignored.

'Trust?' she scoffed, turning her blazing eyes on him. 'You don't even know the meaning of the word,' she threw at him bitterly, thinking of his betrayal.

He grabbed at her arm, pulling her round to face him, and she saw raw, hard anger burning in his eyes and radiating from every pore in his body. And it was all directed at her.

'Listen to me,' he demanded.

'No, I'm through listening to you. You betrayed me; everything I've worked for is in ruins, my whole career gone like that,' she said, clicking her fingers under his nose.

'You'll continue to work here with me. . .'

'You're joking! I'd rather be unemployed than work for you,' she hurled at him, disgusted by the suggestion.

'You don't understand. Let me explain. It was essential that no one knew my plan.'

'Including me?' she asked, saddened all of a sudden that he did not trust her and that he had deliberately misled her.

'Including you. It was for your own good. . .'

'Was it?' she sneered. 'I find that hard to believe.'

His grip on her arm loosened slightly but he still held firm. 'I've been planning it for years.'

'All of it?' she interrupted.

'Yes, when I first went—'

'Every single thing meticulously planned, down to the last detail. . .' she goaded, his temper, which had previously worried her, now only serving to fuel her own.

'Yes. It had to be like that—' he began, straining to control his anger, but Vanessa cut in again, trapping him in his own web.

'Including our engagement? Our lovemaking?' She nearly choked on the word and she turned her face away so that he could not see the tears that were shining in her eyes.

'What?' His hand pinched into her soft skin at her accusation. 'How can you possibly think that?' he asked.

'Very easily,' she said, blinking away her tears and facing him again, sparing him none of the contempt she felt. 'You came up with the idea of a phoney engagement after we met John Haven. . .' She paused as she saw the shock register momentarily in his eyes. 'It's true, isn't it?' she blazed. 'He was part of it, wasn't he? That's why you came with me—I was getting too close to the truth.'

'Yes, John Haven did purchase shares on my behalf and put me in touch with other ex-employees, and I was nervous that if you knew the truth you'd tell Robert,' he told her carefully.

'Yes, I would have,' she said emphatically. 'That's what I was employed to do. So you pretended we were working together—you cheated me, betrayed me, and even made love to me. . .that's really sick.' She shook herself free of his grasp as a bitter taste scorched the back of her throat.

'That's not true. Yes, I did want to prevent you from telling Robert but I do love you. You have to believe that.'

'I'll never believe anything you say ever again,' she said. 'All you care about is getting control of the Knight Corporation. I merely helped you.'

For a moment they both said nothing as they faced each other, locked in an angry silence.

'That's not true. I'd give up everything for you,' he told her, but the sincerity in his tone was wasted on Vanessa, who was still hurting too much to appreciate it.

'Sorry to intrude, but Mr Robert Searle has called a meeting in his office now,' came the efficient voice of Vanessa's secretary, before she disappeared just as quickly as she'd arrived.

'I think it would be better if we arrived separately,' Vanessa said as coolly as she could. Her heart was thudding against her chest and she turned away from him to collect her papers.

'I meant what I said, Vanessa. I do love you—more than anything,' said Ryan as he left.

Vanessa waited a few moments before following him, determinedly ignoring the heartfelt declaration that he had made. But she so much wanted to trust him, to believe what he had said. . .

She paused at the solid oak door of the boardroom, her pulse leaping as she envisaged the reception she was about to receive. Then she braced herself, opened the door and walked in. Robert was seated at the top of the table, flanked by Ryan and Grandmother Searle.

He stared at her, his eyes dark and troubled. The rest of the chairs were taken up by other members of the board.

Their eyes all fixed on her, full of unspoken disapproval and distrust; the only sign of welcome was a smile that twitched at the corners of Ryan's mouth but she ignored it and fixed her gaze firmly on Robert. She slid as silently as she could into her chair.

For a few moments there was silence, before Grandmother Searle barked, 'Well, now we have finally cleared up who has been buying up Knight shares, perhaps, Ryan, you'll be good enough to tell us why and how.' Her tone was still faintly dismissive; she spoke as if he were an errant schoolboy and she a headmistress.

'The how is simple enough. Contrary to popular opinion, I was not frittering away my life on a paradise island,' he said, his eyes flashing to Vanessa as he spoke, but she lowered her eyes so that she did not have to see the accusation there. 'I was very busy following the stock markets; I carefully invested my allowance from the company till I was in a position to acquire Knight shares,' he admitted, enjoying the stunned look on Robert's face.

'For what reason?' his grandmother asked, hating the fact that he had taken centre stage and had made fools of them all.

'I wanted revenge,' he said, then paused, fixing his eyes on Vanessa, again his silence forcing her to look up and face him. 'I wanted to take this company from you as you and this company had taken everything from me—and by that I mean my parents and my childhood,' he said, his voice holding an odd mixture of contempt and weariness.

'I thought I wanted revenge more than anything else in my life but I was wrong—there is something more important to me now than this place,' he confessed.

'Miss Mann,' scorned Robert in disgust, and Ryan glared at him.

'Yes, Vanessa. She knew nothing about this; she is an innocent victim like the rest of you. I kept the truth from her. It was easy at first—she was so prim and proper, with no sense of fun. . .' he told them.

Vanessa scowled at him but he continued with his confession. 'I told her the engagement was a ruse, but I wasn't entirely honest. You see, I did care for her, wanted her, but I knew she'd never accept me; she saw me as a wastrel, a womaniser—thanks to you, Robert,' he added bitterly. 'I was wrong. I should have been honest with her right from the start but I wasn't. I didn't want to hurt her and now I have and I've realised that all this just isn't worth it; it no longer holds the same interest for me.'

Robert gave a snort of derision by way of a response, which incensed Ryan. He leant across the table and grabbed at his cousin's lapels. 'That's the truth,' he growled, his eyes blazing, and Robert smiled weakly.

'All right, if that's what you say,' he agreed readily, and Ryan released his grip, dropping him back into his chair in disgust.

Vanessa stared, mesmerised, at the scene. She was still trying to fathom what Ryan had said and her heart was beating rapidly as she waited to hear more to reassure herself that she had not misheard him.

'Have you any idea what type of family she comes

from?' sneered his grandmother, seeing the power base
she had built up crumbling at her feet. She looked at
Vanessa as she spoke, her eyes gleaming maliciously.
'Because I do, and if you knew the truth I think you'd
find your love failing you.' She smiled cruelly, her thin
lips taut.

'I have had the pleasure of meeting Vanessa's stepfather,' he informed his grandmother, who was clearly
stunned. 'Vanessa, like me, has managed to overcome
her bad start in life, and that's probably another reason
why I love her,' he said.

Vanessa's head shot up. She had definitely heard it that
time; he'd actually said it—no, announced it to everyone. Her heart soared but she was still unable to speak
as she struggled with all that had gone between them.

'So what are your plans for the company?' snapped
his grandmother, refusing to acknowledge what he had
said.

'I have none; I've told you, I've lost all interest.' His
voice had softened and he turned his attention back to
Vanessa. She could feel everyone's eyes on her yet she
had only one point of interest.

'I think I'll take a holiday first. . .' He paused, his
eyes still fixed on Vanessa in a silent plea, and she felt
the familiar tug of attraction. 'I have a lot to think
about.' There was sorrow in his voice and he cast a
small smile at her.

She stared at him as he shuffled his papers together
and rose to his feet. There was silence, everyone
watching his every move; no one moved or spoke.
Vanessa was in complete turmoil. His words echoed
through her mind as her eyes followed him to the door.
He looked so dejected, so beaten. . . For a moment she

sat frozen to the spot but as he opened the door and
she saw that he was going she suddenly knew she
couldn't let him, that deep down inside she did trust
him, did want him, did love him.

Her words and actions became one fluid movement
as she rushed after him.

'Ryan,' she called, and he turned, his face breaking
into a wonderful smile as he flung his arms open wide
to catch her, and their bodies locked together and they
held onto each other as if they would never let go.

Vanessa lifted herself up from the hot sand and raised
her arm across her face to shield her eyes from the
bright sunshine.

'It looks good,' she mused as she studied the beautiful
landscape painting that Ryan was totally involved in.

'You think so?' he asked doubtfully, a paintbrush
clenched between his teeth.

'Aren't all "lollipop" paintings?' she teased, falling
back on to the sand to soak up more sun. 'Why did you
never tell me you were the painter?' she asked sleepily.

'After reading that profile I realised it was the only
bit of information about me you didn't have. I wanted
to keep it a secret,' he told her, fixing his eyes back on
his work. 'Everyone assumed I spent my year in France
being a playboy; however, I was actually working very
hard at developing my artistic skills,' he informed her
smugly.

'So, like Gaugin, you decided to escape to a desert
island and paint.'

'He was married with children.'

'You're married now,' she reminded him with a smile.

He flopped down at the side of her and stroked her

face. 'Aren't I the lucky one?' he crooned, his warm breath gentle on her face. 'And I'm working on the children aspect,' he added, his voice dropping an octave and becoming deep and husky.

'Obviously not hard enough.' Vanessa smiled, turning on her side to face him, her eyes molten pools of invitation, her lips parting softly.

'You're a wicked woman,' he said with a grin as he pulled her to him.

'The first time I came here you referred to me as the snake in the garden of Eden,' she recalled, with amusement sparking in her eyes, and she pressed her body suggestively against him.

'Now I consider you more like Eve,' he said as he trailed his hand down the length of her quivering body. She moaned slightly, enjoying the sensation. 'Let's go up to the house,' he suggested, but Vanessa shook her head.

'I'm happy here, very comfortable.' She pushed her warm body up against him, planting a soft kiss on his lips.

'Here?' Ryan asked in disbelief.

'Why not?' Vanessa asked, her hand already teasing the waistband of his shorts.

'You've changed, Vanessa,' he said proudly, and he rolled over on top of her, pinning her body to the warm ground.

'Aren't you glad?'

'Very,' he admitted as he pressed a hot kiss to her lips, and their bodies melted together. Like Adam and Eve, they were lost in their own paradise. . .

MILLS & BOON®

Next Month's Romances

♡

Each month you can choose from a wide variety of romance novels from Mills & Boon. Below are the new titles to look out for next month from the Presents and Enchanted series.

Presents™

Enchanted™

'Happy' Greetings!

Would you like to win a year's supply of Mills & Boon® books?
Well you can and they're free! Simply complete the
competition below and send it to us by 31st August 1997. The
first five correct entries picked after the closing date will each
win a year's subscription to the Mills & Boon series of their
choice. What could be easier?

ACSPPMTHYHARSI

_ _ _ _ _ _ _ _ _ _ _ _

TPHEEYPSARA

_ _ _ _ _ _ _ _ _

RAHIHPYBDYTAP

_ _ _ _ _ _ _ _ _ _ _ _

NHMYRTSPAAPNERUY

_ _ _ _ _ _ _ _ _ _ _ _

DYVLTEPYAANINSEPAH

_ _ _ _ _ _ _ _ _ _ _ _ _

YAYPNAHPEREW

_ _ _ _ _ _ _ _ _

DMHPYAHRYOSETPA

_ _ _ _ _ _ _ _ _ _ _

VRHYPNARSAEYNPIA

_ _ _ _ _ _ _ _ _ _ _ _

Please turn over for details of how to enter ☞

How to enter...

There are eight jumbled up greetings overleaf, most of which you will probably hear at some point throughout the year. Each of the greetings is a 'happy' one, i.e. the word 'happy' is somewhere within it. All you have to do is identify each greeting and write your answers in the spaces provided. Good luck!

When you have unravelled each greeting don't forget to fill in your name and address in the space provided and tick the Mills & Boon® series you would like to receive if you are a winner. Then simply pop this page into an envelope (you don't even need a stamp) and post it today. Hurry—competition ends 31st August 1997.

Mills & Boon 'Happy' Greetings Competition
FREEPOST, Croydon, Surrey, CR9 3WZ

Please tick the series you would like to receive if you are a winner

Presents™ ❑   Enchanted™ ❑   Medical Romance™ ❑
Historical Romance™ ❑   Temptation® ❑

Are you a Reader Service Subscriber?   Yes ❑   No ❑

Ms/Mrs/Miss/Mr _____
(BLOCK CAPS PLEASE)

Address _____

_____

_____ Postcode _____

(I am over 18 years of age)

One application per household. Competition open to residents of the UK and Ireland only.
You may be mailed with other offers from other reputable companies as a result of this application. If you would prefer not to receive such offers, please tick box.   ❑

mps MAILING PREFERENCE SERVICE   DMA   C7B